vol 1, issue 3

EDITED BY
RICK OLLERMAN

Magazine Copyright © 2018 by Down & Out Books
Individual Story Copyrights © 2018 by Individual Authors, except

"Death in the Pasig" originally appeared in the March 1930 issue of *Black Mask* magazine (Vol. 13, No. 1). Copyright 1930 by Popular Publications, Inc. Copyright renewed 1957 and assigned to Steeger Properties, LLC. All Rights Reserved.

All rights reserved. No part of the book may be reproduced in any form or by any electronic or mechanical means, including information storage and retrieval systems, without permission in writing from the publisher, except by a reviewer who may quote brief passages in a review.

Down & Out Books
3959 Van Dyke Road, Suite 265
Lutz, FL 33558
DownAndOutBooks.com

The characters and events in this book are fictitious. Any similarity to real persons, living or dead, is coincidental and not intended by the author.

Cover photo © by Mason Sanders
Cover design by Lance Wright

ISBN: 1-946502-99-5
ISBN-13: 978-1-946502-99-5

CONTENTS

A Few Clues From the Editor
Rick Ollerman — 1

Kickback
Peter Sellers — 5

The Wheel Has Come Full Circle
Patricia Abbott — 16

Adam Raised a Cain
Frank Zafiro — 27

Hey, Hockey Puck
Robert J. Randisi — 44

Placed in Evidence (non-fiction)
J. Kingston Pierce — 71

FEATURE STORY
Three-Star Sushi
Barry Lancet — 80

Sunday Morning, Saturday Night
Art Taylor — 106

A Few Cents a Word
Rick Ollerman — 110

Death in the Pasig
Raoul Whitfield — 114

Bear Trap
Jim Wilsky — 128

Texas Sundown
Michael Bracken — 147

Titan
S.A. Solomon — 153

A Few Clues From the Editor
Rick Ollerman

I was working on a piece about a writer who once sold between seventy and eighty *million* books in his three decades-plus year career the other week. Eighty. Million. Books. This author wrote from the early fifties well past the time of my "formative" years of reading (though those never really end, do they?). He wrote up until he passed away in the mid-1980s, a time when I was jumping out of airplanes and attending the engineering school at the University of Minnesota, not thinking much of nebulous concepts like "the future." I didn't even have a well-defined idea of what an engineer actually *did,* let alone whether or not I actually wanted to be one.

Anyway, if I told you this author's name right now, you might very well say, "Who?" And if you didn't, if you happened to be familiar with the man's books but not the *works*, you might say instead, "Wasn't he the one with all those sexy covers?" (One of those guys, anyway.) So the publisher's strategy of "sex sells" worked, at least on the paperback side, which was where this particular author spent his career.

A more discerning collector may even ask, "Isn't he the one that had all those wonderful Robert McGinnis covers?" And you'd be correct again: the American editions of his books were published by NAL's paperback arm, Signet, and hundreds of his paperbacks were graced by McGinnis's small masterworks. And anyway, all of this misses the point...

A writer who becomes *that* popular, a writer who can sell *that* many books worldwide, who can be *translated into more than thirty languages*, a man whose career could go nearly forgotten in less time than it took him to actually build that career—well, frankly, this scares the pants off me. When a writer sells their first book, my first piece of advice—if asked—is a bit of a downer. "Welcome to obscurity," I tell them. "Now sit down and write another one. That's the only thing in this business you can control." It's rare that we have a Harper Lee who can be a successful writer with one book. I've seen people who have written one book and spent years and years trying to sell and market it. Is that really what you want to do, or do you want to be a writer? Then there's no way around it, you have to sit down and write...

But this writer is far from the only one to suffer this same fate. It wouldn't be difficult to track down the piece I'm talking about if you really want to read more about what who this particular gentleman is. Should be out in book form in a few months.

But recently we lost a fine writer and an even better man, our feature writer for the last issue, Bill Crider. His story, "Tell the Bees," won't be his last story published but I believe it was the last story he actually wrote. When we first talked about doing a story for the magazine, he thought it was time he brought back his old character Truman Smith. After a while, though, Bill told me he wasn't coming up with an idea and he went back to the original plan, which was a new story featuring Blacklin County's own Sheriff Dan Rhodes.

Bill often professed his admiration for his favorite writer, Harry Whittington. Whittington was another well-known author of more than two hundred books. Once nicknamed "King of the Paperbacks," Whittington now shares a fate closer to that of the gentleman I talked about above. (At the time of his death, in Whittington's library were a number of the other writer's paperbacks, all with signature McGinnis covers.) Bill regretted that he and Harry had never met but they corresponded and Whittington sent Bill some valuable hardcover books from early in his career. I knew Bill and I know Harry's family, and both writers were gentleman of the first order. I regret they didn't get to meet in person, too.

Late last year, after Bill told me that his medical options had suddenly become limited, I asked Harry's daughter (who sadly passed away in late November) if I could do something for Bill I thought he might find special. I had in my possession an unpublished manuscript by Harry, actually the last book by "Harry Whittington" before he became "Ashley Carter" and took over a bestselling series from an aging Lance Horner.

As best as I could determine, no one other than Harry had ever read the book. Harry had been in the habit of reading his manuscripts to his wife, Kathryn, as part of his process, but once it was written, it does not appear that it would have been read by anyone else.

With Harriet's permission, I carefully copied each page by hand and sent it off to Bill at his home in Alvin, Texas. Although he'd never had the chance to meet his favorite writer, he was at least able to be the first person to read a book by his favorite writer, one that nobody else had ever read.

Another "forgotten" writer, a man I think of as the James Lee Burke of the science fiction/fantasy genre, Jack Vance, mentioned in his autobiography that he enjoyed reading Bill's Sheriff Dan Rhodes series. Bill had no idea Vance was even aware of him and that mention took him completely by surprise. It led to some pleasant communication with the then-blind writer in the months before Vance himself passed away.

I've been hopping around here this issue, throwing out anecdotes and intersecting some of them with Bill Crider and other writers who have turned up overlooked. There's no doubt that if you were to look further into Bill's past (or could somehow peer into his own encyclopedic mind) you'd find many more. But I don't want to.

Just like I don't want Bill's work to fall into that most unjust of literary crevices. Quality isn't always the newest thing, it isn't always the subject of the glitziest media campaign, or the seed of the next Tom Cruise movie. It could have been that series, that one there, those twenty-one Sheriff Rhodes novels set in fictional Blacklin County with its cast of distinctive supporting characters. The supporting folks that propped up Sheriff Rhodes and made readers want his home to be real place. Bill gave his county and its residents a gentle warmth (unless they were the bad guys) that could be as comfortable and familiar as a pair of wool socks in front of the wood stove in winter.

Bill Crider was a writer's writer. He won a lot of awards, and was nominated for many others. Funny that I never heard him mention any of that.

We have the new guys, the new writers coming up in the ranks. We need them or we'd all be in trouble. But we can't afford to forget the footsteps in which they follow, the shoulders they're standing on, the inspiration they've hopefully gleaned from the bestsellers and mid-listers alike, and the writers that inspired not only themselves, but other writers similar to themselves, to put pen to paper in the first place.

Don't forget those writers just because they're older than you are. Don't forget Bill Crider.

For Bill Crider, 1941—2018
Who could have said all of this so much better

Rick Ollerman

Peter and I met at last year's Bouchercon in Toronto where he was engaging in another one of his literary pursuits, antiquarian bookselling. He had some beautiful books by E. Phillips Oppenheim, "The Prince of Storytellers" (who easily belongs in the category of "forgotten" writers I mentioned above). They're now my books but Peter held a few back, slyly realizing he could read them first and still sell them to me later. What I didn't know at the time was how successful and wonderful an author he was, with many appearances in Alfred Hitchcock's *and* Ellery Queen's Mystery Magazines, *among others, to his credit. He slipped me a copy of an anthology of his work which I ended up devouring when I got home. I asked him for a story, and here it is. He tells me he has another anthology coming out next year, and yes, I'll be first in line. His terse and clear style is one of those deceptive things that most writers know how hard it is to pull off. Peter makes it look easy.*

Kickback
Peter Sellers

They say that people from Montreal drive like maniacs. The first time I drove with him, I figured Gilbert was the guy they had in mind. His dad owned a printing business, and Gil used his knowledge of printing terminology to lie his way into a job as print production manager at the ad agency I worked for. It took about two days for them to figure out he was utterly unqualified, but for reasons beyond understanding, they didn't fire him. They made him an account executive. I guess they figured if he could sell himself into a job he couldn't do, he could sell clients ads that didn't work. If they'd canned him, probably none of this would have happened.

Gil walked into my office on his first day, grinning. "Have you written a novel yet?" he asked.

My mind said, *Fuck off*, but the part of me that likes to get along with people said, "Yeah. It's shit, but I wrote one."

Gil asked the same question to Lynne, the other copywriter, who shared the office with me.

She laughed and shook her head. "You must have some work to do," she said. Later, Gil confessed to me that he did have work to do but had no idea how to do it.

Lynne responded to many questions by laughing and shaking her head. She did the same thing the first time I asked her out. Then she said, "You don't make enough money. And you live with your parents."

"Not much longer," I said, stung by the truth that I had not realized was public knowledge. "A buddy and I just got a place. I'm moving out in two weeks."

"Great. What about the money part?"

Eleven grand a year seemed like a lot to me, but not everyone saw it that way.

Lynne's desk and mine faced each other with a five-foot partition between. It meant I could not see her when we were seated, but it was not high enough to block the clatter of typewriter keys or the smoke from Lynne's constant cigarettes.

The partition was also the perfect height for me to lean against and talk with her when we weren't typing. She always left her top few buttons undone and from that angle I could look down the front of her shirt. This was the moment that I knew she was interested in me, even though she hadn't said anything.

What made her interest even more obvious was the photograph. She had returned from a vacation at an adults-only resort in the Caribbean where she had gone with a jingle house sales rep she was seeing and some of his high-powered ad agency friends.

"How was the trip?" I asked.

She laughed. "Good. It was great just to be able to kick back and relax." She took out a four-by-six color print. In the photo, she was standing up to her knees in the turquoise water next to a man I recognized as the creative director of a major agency. He was holding a drink and she was turned sideways to him with her arms around his neck and her lips against his cheek. She had a cigarette between the fingers of her right hand and she was wearing a white T-shirt. The water stretched off to the horizon, uninterrupted by boat or any other sign of life, and the sky was cloudless. It took a second for me to realize she was wearing nothing other than the T-shirt, which came to just above her waist. When I handed the photo back, Lynne gave me a look that seemed to be asking what I thought.

"It looks very relaxing," I said.

She laughed in a way that made me uncomfortable, but it was obviously just to hide her feelings. There was no way she would show me that photo if she wasn't interested.

The first time I drove with Gil was eye-opening, though I reckon Jackie spent the time with his eyes closed.

Gil had a Honda Civic, which was a very small car. Jackie, our boss, had to take his Corvette in for service, and I didn't have a vehicle, so he asked Gil to drive us to a meeting. I squeezed into the tiny back seat with Jackie riding shotgun. I was smart enough to do up my seatbelt but Jackie was more cavalier about things like that. Gil lurched towards the exit of the parking lot. A line of vehicles waiting for a light blocked access to the street. Gil turned onto the sidewalk, drove past the end of the line of cars, and bounced over the curb onto the road. I watched Jackie's head smack off the roof. "Jesus," he said, rubbing his head then grabbing the dashboard with both hands as Gil roared down the street. Six blocks later, Jackie yelled, "Stop the fucking car. Now." I was surprised at the outburst as the whole thing stuck me as fun and amusing.

Gil pulled to the curb and Jackie climbed out, slamming the door with a violence that shook the vehicle. He raised his arm to hail a cab. "I guess we'll meet him there," Gil said, not put out at all.

When Jackie hired me, I assumed that he and his partner, Alan Thomas, knew what they were doing. I figured that everyone at the agency would be competent. My first clue to the contrary was when Jackie told me I had the job. He asked me if I could bring my own typewriter. I was smart enough to say no, and they supplied a stiff and noisy Remington upright.

I was rolling in a sheet of paper on my first day when Alan came and stood next to me. "So you're the asshole who wanted to get into advertising," he said.

Jackie had no previous advertising experience beyond watching commercials on TV. Alan knew a bit more than Jackie. He'd worked as ad manager for a second-rate discount retail chain that had gone out of business a couple of years before. The rest of us were basically enthusiastic amateurs who were willing to work cheap.

The two agency art directors, Kent and Bev, sat together in an open area of the office. They spent most of their time hunched over their drafting tables, assembling print ads for shipping to magazines and newspapers. In those days, sheets of typeset copy arrived from the type house and the art directors used scalpels to cut the sheets apart and to make any necessary changes. Spacing was refined. Words were moved. Headlines were shifted. Hot wax was used to stick the copy to the art boards that were sent out for photo-static reproduction once approved by the client.

I was talking with Bev one day when Jackie came over and picked up Kent's scalpel. "I need to borrow this," Jackie said.

He used the blade to slice a hangnail off one of his fingers. "That's better," he said, putting the scalpel back and walking away.

I must have looked surprised because Kent said, "He does that all the time. I think he uses them to pick his teeth."

The next time I asked Lynne out, I had come back from lunch a little drunk. Lynne was smoking and reading the paper. I gave her a charming smile. "Let's go out on Friday night," I said. "We can go dancing. I got my own place now."

"You're sharing it," she said with a laugh. "And did you get a raise that I don't know about?"

"No, but I got a car."

"Yeah," she said, "I've seen it. Although just barely through that smokescreen it throws up. I mean a real car."

The car needed new piston rings and burned oil, causing a blue haze when I drove, but it really wasn't that bad. The good news was that she still hadn't given me a flat out no.

* * *

One day, the marketing manager of our shoe store client called to complain about a brochure that we had created. "Pure puffery," she said. Gil and I took the initiative and drove to her office to resolve the situation.

We spent half an hour defending our work, and then grudgingly agreed to make changes. When we got back, Jackie called us into his office. He was opening his mail with a scalpel. As soon as we were through the door, he pointed the blade at us and started yelling. "What the hell were you idiots thinking? Never go to see her without me. In fact, never go to see any client without me. In fact, never go to see any client. Period. Do you know what I had to go through to calm her down, you morons?" He went on like that for some time. I had never been on the receiving end of Jackie's temper and it shook me. I felt frightened and angry. Finally, he told us to get the hell out of his office. A day later his outburst made sense.

Around two o'clock the following afternoon, Jackie was on the phone, behind closed doors. His voice was raised, and it sounded like he was making an impassioned pitch that was not going well. The receiver slammed down suddenly and sharply. I was about to knock on his door when the smashing started. It was loud and persistent, coupled with the sound of breaking plastic, Jackie swearing all the while. When the noise stopped, Jackie stormed out of his office. He found the office manager and said, "I need a new phone, Iris. Mine doesn't work anymore." His voice was surprisingly calm.

I looked in and the floor was covered with smashed plastic.

"Jesus," I said to Lynne. "That can't be good."

The call had been from our biggest client, firing us. The next day another piece of business did the same thing. The morning after that, a third of the staff was fired, including Lynne. Gil kept his job but they laid me off and then hired me back on a freelance basis. I guess they thought that would save them money. In fact, my new rates gave me a raise.

A few days after the mass firing, I called Lynne at home. "You can go out with me now," I said. "I'm making more money than you."

"Don't make me come down there and hit you," she said. "Call me when you have a good car."

In an attempt to salvage the agency, Jackie and Alan merged with Ryan Clark, a friend who owned the recording studio we used for radio spots.

Ryan had a few clients of his own. His answer to every advertising problem was to use radio, preferably in the form of a bouncy jingle. He wrote the commercials, produced them in his studio, composed the music, played piano on the recording sessions, and even did the voiceovers. His background in radio news made every spot he read sounded like a recap of the day's headlines.

After the merger, our use of jingles increased beyond common sense. Ryan believed that a jingle could boost sales for a custom drapery company by repeating the company's phone number over and over. This approach had worked well for a chain of pizza joints. Ryan was certain it would work for curtains, too, as if people ordered sheers and vertical blinds as frequently as they ordered a double pepperoni with extra cheese.

Jackie fought the idea in several heated discussions to no avail. I was puzzled by the client's willingness to buy a campaign that was so ill-advised. Ryan must have been a heck of a salesman.

Three weeks later, we won a modest piece of new business. A brief article about the acquisition appeared in one of the trade rags. The client was quoted as saying, "We picked the agency more for what Ryan Clark knows about radio than for what they know about advertising." Jackie read this and destroyed his bookcase by kicking it repeatedly with the bottom of his foot, leaving the shelves canted and books and splintered wood on the carpet. Gil and I got a hammer and some finishing nails and did our best to repair the damage, but it was always rickety after that. Putting a cup of coffee on top of it was an act of faith.

Ryan frequently told people in the office to do things that made no sense. One plan involved promoting our car stereo client's products by having thieves talk about why they liked to steal them. He was trying to arrange interviews with convicted felons. He wanted me to write sample scripts. I went to talk with Jackie and Alan.

"This is insane," I said, sitting on the sofa next to Alan.

"Jesus Christ," Alan said.

Jackie corrected him. "Jesus wept."

I was hoping they'd have more to say about it when Ryan stuck his head in the door. "Have you written the scripts yet?" he asked, staring at me.

"I'm not doing them. It's a bad idea."

Ryan tipped his head to one side and gazed at me as if I were an unusual specimen. "I want the scripts. First thing tomorrow."

"Look, Ryan," said Alan, "we all agree on this. It's not happening."

Ryan glared at his two partners. "This is my client. I brought him in. And we deal with my clients my way." He looked at me again. "Tomorrow. First thing." He walked away.

Seconds later, Jackie picked up his coffee cup and hurled it at the doorway. It was half full, and cold coffee flew across the sofa, Alan, and me. The cup hit the doorframe and smashed, shards of porcelain flying across the room. He put on his coat and left.

I was stunned. Alan and I sat in silence briefly, until Ryan reappeared in the doorway. "What happened? Did someone throw something at me? Was someone trying to kill me?" He looked around the office in a frantic manner.

"Ryan," Alan said, "go home."

Ryan looked around one last time and went. Alan stood, brushing at the coffee stain on his trousers. "Remember, kid," he said, "you're the asshole who wanted to get into advertising."

I assumed that most of the agency's accounts stayed on because of friendships, one of the partners knowing a CEO or an advertising director. Competence didn't seem to enter into it. Then, late one Friday afternoon, I was at my desk after everyone else had gone. I was editing some copy by pen and being very quiet. When the shouting started I peeked out and saw Jackie waving a piece of paper and walking across the office towards Ryan.

"What the hell is this?" Jackie yelled.

Ryan took the paper, glanced at it, and handed it back. "It's a canceled check," he said calmly. "That's how we keep the account."

"Jesus." They went into Jackie's office, which adjoined mine.

The voices through the wall were muffled but clear enough. "We're fighting to make our nut," Jackie said, "and you're giving away what little profit there is."

"Think that through, Jackie. What I'm doing is investing part of the profit to make sure we keep the rest. Do you think if these checks stopped going out the ones from the client would keep coming in? It's been working this way for years. Stay out of it."

There was more, but that was the important part.

Soon after, the checks did stop because Ryan came up with an alternative. Ryan's car was in the shop one day when he saw Gil standing in reception, yacking to anyone who would listen, looking like he had nothing to do.

"Get your keys, Gilbert," Ryan said. "You're driving me to a meeting." Ryan had never been in Gil's car before and may not have believed the stories.

"Do I get mileage?" Gil asked.

"You get to keep your job."

When I asked Gil later, he told me he had dropped Ryan off in front of a café in the west end. As he waited for a break in traffic so he could pull away, he saw the client sitting at a table in the window. Ryan went in and sat across from him. Why, I wondered, were they meeting on the far side of town, away from both the agency and the client's office? And why in a coffee shop? Both of them preferred martinis and places like Barberien's Steak House.

A month later, Ryan needed a lift again. Gil grabbed his keys. "Ready when you are," he said.

"Not on your fucking life," Ryan said. He pointed at me. "You got wheels now, right?" He started towards the door and I followed.

Ryan went back to the coffee shop and met the client at a table in the window. I made a quick U-turn and pulled over. From the far side of the road, I watched Ryan take an envelope from his pocket and hand it to the client.

It wasn't hard to put together. Just like Jackie asked, Ryan had stopped giving checks to the client and had switched to an envelope full of cash. The money was probably being funneled out of the recording studio, so Jackie wouldn't see it leave right away. It would show up eventually, and there'd be problems, but for a while this would keep the peace and the account.

I drove Ryan the next month, too, and followed him the month after that. The pattern was always the same.

I watched Jackie on kickback days, looking for indications that he suspected anything. By that point, though, he looked at Ryan with anger or contempt most of the time. It was hard to pick out days that were worse than others. Ryan seemed oblivious, smiling and whistling around the office, but you could feel the tension.

In May, I left the office before Ryan did and waited outside the coffee shop. He did not show up. Neither did the client. I waited half an hour.

Ryan was at his desk when I got back. He was on the phone giving his hearty salesman's laugh.

"Has Ryan been laughing like that all day?" I asked his secretary who rolled her eyes.

It was clear that nothing was wrong or he wouldn't be so jolly. Later, as I was pouring a coffee, Ryan asked, "Big plans for the weekend?"

"Nothing special. You?"

"Golfing with the client," he laughed. "Betcha I win some money off him."

I thought it'd be the other way round, the envelope changing hands before they got to the second tee.

After work that evening, I went out for a beer with a couple of friends at a bar down the street. I left my briefcase in my office and went back to get it before driving home.

The office was at the far side of a closed-off courtyard. The front door could not be seen from the street. It wasn't until I entered the courtyard that I saw the office lights still on. No big deal. Sometimes people forgot. But the door was unlocked, which was not normal. The place was silent. I walked in quietly in case of a burglar. Instead, Jackie was standing in Ryan's office.

There was a lot of blood. Ryan was on the floor, drenched and not moving. Except for his deep and steady breathing, Jackie was not moving either. His clothes were less bloody but still past cleaning. His hands were bloody, too, and the scalpel he held.

"Jesus," I said. "What the fuck?"

Jackie looked at me sadly. "I lost my temper."

"Put down the blade, Jackie." I didn't think I was in danger, but there was no point taking the risk.

Jackie looked at the scalpel and let it fall.

"What happened?"

"I told him to stop with the kickbacks. I gave him lots of chances. He laughed."

"Yeah, that laugh was pretty fucking annoying." I didn't bother to pretend I didn't know what had been going on.

"The amount was going up. The client threatened to take away the account. Ryan was paying him more."

"And you killed him for that?"

"I told him to stop. I lost my temper. He laughed."

"Okay," I said, "here's what we do." Jackie was in no condition to take the initiative. "Don't touch anything." His prints were all over the office so that was no problem, but bloody prints would raise eyebrows. I got some plastic wrap from the kitchen. "Wrap the scalpel in this and hand it to me. Handle first." In a day or two, I'd take the ferry to the Island and drop it in the middle of the lake.

I picked up a promotional T-shirt from a radio station, and a pair of rubber gloves from under the sink. "Put these on."

"I want to wash my hands," he said.

"No. Put on the gloves." I took him to the front door. "Go outside. I'm going to lock the door. You smash the glass and unlock it. Understand?"

He nodded. "What do I smash it with?"

"Find a rock or a brick or something."

The rock bounced off the door a couple of times before the glass shattered and Jackie came in. I was grateful that the courtyard hid the office from view, though the sound of the rock did echo. But no one came to investigate.

"Okay. Now follow me."

We went back to Ryan's office. His top desk drawer was locked. I broke it open. The envelope was there as I'd expected. There was so cash it bulged in my pocket. I left the drawer hanging open.

"I want a beer," Jackie said. "Let's go to a bar."

"Don't be an idiot. Here's what you do unless you want to spend a long time in Kingston. Go home. Get rid of those clothes. Burn them. Clean yourself up. Keep your mouth shut about everything that happened here. And keep your temper under control."

"What about this mess?"

"We leave it. When he doesn't come home, they're gonna start looking. For sure they will when he misses his tee-off time tomorrow. Now get out of here."

"What about the money?"

"I'm keeping it."

Jackie took out his car keys and started for the door.

"Hang on," I said. "Hold out your hand." It was shaking badly. "You're not taking your car. In that thing you'll be all over the road and if the cops see a black guy all bloody driving a 'Vette it's not gonna end well."

Jackie nodded. "I'll take a cab."

I marveled at how dense he was. "No you're not. You get in a cab all bloody like that anywhere within five miles of here and you're fucked." I reached into my pocket and gave him my keys. "Take my car. It's a piece of shit and it won't go fast enough for you to do any damage. No one'll pay any attention."

He dropped his keys on the desk and took mine. "Have a good weekend," I said.

On Monday, if he hadn't done something stupid, I'd talk to Jackie about what was in this for me. And there had to be some way to make money out of the client. I figured he'd want all those years of kickbacks kept quiet.

Before leaving, I called Lynne. "Hey," I said, "do you want to go out for a drink tonight?" Before she could say no, I added, "I got lots of money." I glanced at the keys on Jackie's desk. "And I got a real nice car."

Patricia, or Patti, Abbott, has been a consummate writer of short fiction for many years. Literate, suspenseful, and with the ability to transport her readers into urban and rural worlds that are layered and never quite what they seem. Her stories take place in the seams of the world that we find ourselves inhabiting every day; they're not in any bigger than life, exaggerated world. She writes about the places we work in, that we drive through, places that we ourselves already know, relationships we make for ourselves. Her work has either won or been nominated for every major award, including the Mystery Writers of America's Edgar Award. Her two novels, published by Polis Books, have received wonderful notices, and her next offering, a short story collection called I Bring Sorrow & Other Stories of Transgression, *should be on shelves just about the time you read this.*

The Wheel Has Come Full Circle
Patricia Abbott

When he heard the familiar laugh, Harry Eberly was seated on a patio in Wellfleet on the Cape. Tina was describing a recent victory at work and Harry was listening in the way of long-married husbands, taking in enough to nod sympathetically in the correct places but not enough to feel suicidal. The remains of their meal had been snatched away moments earlier by an overly efficient busboy, and Harry was primarily occupied with grieving the loss of his last two scallops, something he'd spaced out carefully, resisting the desire to gobble them down. He'd turned his head to watch a passing dessert cart, and it was then the theft occurred. Having been allocated only six scallops, it seemed unjust he'd sacrificed two to inattention.

It was then he heard the laugh. Prickles of sweat danced beneath his collar as he sought to identify it. Uneasily, he swiveled in his seat. Seated three tables away was the wife of his youth: Hannah.

No, that couldn't be, he quickly realized. Too young. Hannah would be the woman across the table. The younger woman, a carbon copy, must be her daughter.

But his Hannah looked wonderful too, luminescent in the fading light. She was leaning in, a smile still warming her face. He turned back in time to appear engrossed in Tina's story, coming to its merciful end.

"Did you see someone you knew?" She was scrutinizing him—looking for some newly committed sin, some fresh grievance she could wield like a sword.

"I thought so. But it wasn't him."

How easily the lie rolled off his tongue. For a moment, he focused entirely on his wife. Her eyes were accusatory pinpricks in the dusk. Turning back seconds later, he watched as Hannah and her daughter rose from their table. A whiff of her perfume—was it Chantilly still—seemed to hover as they passed his table. A flood of memories occupied the remainder of his evening; Tina read the latest Jack Reacher, suffused in only a faint scent of discontent.

After a restless night, Harry rose early, offering to make a trip to the grocery store for fresh bagels. Nodding happily over the top of the *Times,* Tina pushed her half-eaten bowl of Puffins aside.

"Could you pick up some sun block too? Like a fifty?" she asked, picking up a pencil for the crossword. Striding down the street, he passed the boy who'd bussed their table the night before, the family who'd occupied the next blanket at the beach yesterday, the owner of the town's bookshop.

"Enjoying the Richard Ford?" the man called out. Harry nodded. They'd only been here three days but were already regulars. He could be picked out of a lineup, he thought.

Downtown Wellfleet consisted of a string of shops for the tourist trade, restaurants, and a single grocery store. Hannah was coming out the door as he approached. She looked him head-on without a flicker of recognition. Could he have changed that much? Certainly his beard, mustache, and the mid-neck length hair of the nineties were long gone. He was clean-shaven now, had tried the two-day beard look a few years ago but discarded it. The meager span of hair he lay claim to was cropped close. And, of course, he wore contacts. Then he'd sported large, aviator glasses—tinted blue—if he remembered correctly.

Hannah looked nearly the same. She wore a loose-fitting dress and her figure had the same generous proportions it had at twenty-three. Her hair, still long, was a bit gray. He wondered why she didn't touch it up. Tina would have. He watched her walk down the street in her old, unhurried fashion, her ass swishing provocatively. No one had told her she was too old to walk that way, thank God. When she disappeared around the corner, he pushed open the door of the shop and went inside.

The teenager at the battered, knotty-pine counter waited patiently while he considered the extensive selection of bagels. He should've known the kind Tina preferred but was too distracted by his brush with Hannah to come up with it. Poppy seed? Egg? The muffins sitting on the counter looked like tiny grenades, each harboring the necessary grain and fruit to rally an aging boomer's colon.

A grocery list sat on the counter. Reading upside down, he saw the name, *Hannah York*, with an address in Wellfleet scribbled underneath? She must live nearby—or at least summer here. And she'd remarried. He'd given Hannah less than three minute's thought a year for the past twenty-five years, but that didn't lessen the blow. Surely, in a town this small it'd be easy to find her. Forgetting the sun block, he trotted home, overshooting their rental by several blocks as he pondered his past.

Harry Eberly married Hannah Khoury immediately after her graduation from Douglas College in New Brunswick. Harry was in his second year in the graduate program in history at Columbia. As it turned out, he wasn't cut out for the academic life. Increasingly, he found himself straining for originality in his papers and in class discussion. Observations that seemed original and pithy in front of his bathroom mirror or when delivered to an appreciative Hannah seemed trite and pedestrian around the seminar table. Often his comments served only to summarize what other students had already said.

A professor of French military history first made that observation in Harry's second year of study in the privacy of the department's fire escape. Godfrey, smoking his ubiquitous pipe in the cold March winds while holding his plaid hat with one hand and a monstrously heavy table lighter with the other, offered him the necessary impetus for a quick exit from the hell of graduate school.

"There must be something you're better at than this, Eberly. Seek it out."

Harry put out the final cigarette of his life and exited academia with relief. He was better suited to business, he soon found, and after finishing his master's thesis the next semester, found employment on Wall Street. What would have been hell to most of his fellow students was a joy to him. He was wildly successful at making money, a skill his old friends loathed. Whereas they went to art house movies in Princeton and played softball and charades, his new friends played squash and sailed on the weekends. How quickly he forget the old names.

And Hannah? Well, increasingly, her hippie looks and addiction to community theater and dabbling at oil painting didn't play well on Wall Street. As Harry's thoughts turned toward their future children and his progression in the firm, Hannah didn't seem the proper helpmate. She was sure to insist on open classrooms, pen pals in Nicaragua, community gardens, and recycling efforts on some grand scale. The other company wives had abandoned relics like non-tailored clothes, the music of Joni Mitchell, and prosaic beef stews. The oil paint never seemed completely washed from Hannah's hands. Her small talk was never small enough.

Harry and Hannah divorced, the exact timetable was a blur. Soon, he'd found the perfect mate in Tina Li, a new hire in his office. She had both the intensity and drive to suit the nineties. Her career path would line up perfectly with his. And if there were children, well, she'd be excellent in that arena too. Or they could hire someone who was.

Harry dropped the bag of bagels on the kitchen table and set a container of coffee next to it. Tina had disappeared and he used the opportunity to hunt down the map the realtor had given him. It took only seconds to locate Pearson Street. He could be there in minutes. He wasn't sure what he would do after that, but he didn't like to overthink a situation.

Tina appeared dressed for the beach, and he couldn't help but notice how fantastic her figure was. How many women her age could wear a two-piece suit? Of course, not bearing children helped.

Tina and Harry were a wealthy, successful couple but hadn't one damned thing to say to each other.

"Coming to the beach?" Tina asked, loading her bag with the sunbathing essentials of the post-ozone layered world. "Could you get my back?" she asked, turning around and handing him the lotion. Thankfully, she didn't mention his failure to supplement their supply.

For a minute, he considered inviting her into the bedroom. It'd been a long time since they'd had sex in the daytime. Or at night, for that matter. Tina seldom came up for air. Even this brief vacation was unusual for them, their first together in three years. A vacation put stress on a floundering marriage. They didn't have a carefully worked out routine to rely on here. Their little avenues of escape, their various ruses, were difficult to beckon on the terra exotica of Cape Cod. The exposure was pitiless.

"Maybe later," he said. "I was thinking about hitting a few balls before it gets too hot."

Tina sniffed, her way of reminding him they'd agreed not to pursue solitary activities on this vacation. Their therapist suggested this only last week. After much discussion, each had left behind their laptops and briefcases, counting on good weather and the memory of past vacations to see them through. Only his cell phone, hidden in the glove compartment, connected them with the real world. Tina stuffed a final towel in her bag, grabbed the bag of bagels and the beach umbrella, and took off. Less than five feet two and a hundred pounds, she could carry more equipment than a pack mule.

"I'll just be an hour," he called after her.

"That should give you the right amount of time to go fuck yourself."

Pearson Street was a shady side street with a stretch of pines providing a dramatic backdrop to the strikingly modern houses. Apparently, Hannah married well or moved on to something more lucrative than her middle school teaching position. There were just three houses on the unpaved lane. Widely separated, each was carefully angled to provide the maximum in privacy, drama and light. Hannah's address put her in the final house, which looked out on a small body of water. He parked the car and got out. Since there were no cars in the driveway or in the parking area dead ending the street, it seemed safe to poke around. Surreptitiously, he walked to the back of the house.

The clothesline predictably held bathing suits and beach towels. The grounds also boasted a squat dock with both a canoe and rowboat tightly tethered, a sagging badminton net with the worn grass to prove its use, a two-tiered deck with more than a dozen chairs and several tables, an ancient swing set and half a dozen outdoor toys and games. This could have been his had things gone differently. Invitingly untidy, the yard marked the Yorks as an active family. Large windows at the back of the house took advantage of the area's natural beauty. Growing bold, he shaded his eyes and peered inside.

"Can I do anything for you?" the girl from the restaurant patio said, coming out of the house. Once again, she reminded him of the Hannah of his youth. Closer now, he saw her eyes were a different color, her nose a bit more narrow. The voice wasn't Hannah's either, and it was a bit stern right now.

"Oh, sorry," he said, thinking quickly. "Is this the Johnson house? Bob James sent me over to see it." James was the realtor who found their summer rental.

The bristling manner disappeared as the girl visibly relaxed. "No, I'm sorry. We're the Yorks. You must have the wrong street or something. Johnson, you said?"

He took the folded map out of his pocket, pretending to consult it. "Yes, Al and Barb Johnson. I guess I'll give Bob a call and recheck my information. I hope I didn't scare you."

Smiling, she shook her head. "Well. I'd better get back to work then."

He took this as a signal to move on, and after taking a last look at the girl who might have been his daughter but probably wasn't, returned to the car. He watched a moment longer as she donned the helmet under her arm, climbed on a blue bike, and sped down the lane, waving to a small boy on a scooter.

He sat there for a few minutes, hoping Hannah might return. When this didn't happen, he drove slowly back to his cottage, changed into his swimsuit and joined his wife at the beach. She lay face down on the blanket, glistening with what must be the last of the sun block. For a small woman, Tina had a sizable chest. It seemed to him it'd be rather like lying on beach balls, but he supposed that must not be the case. Breasts must either squash down or obligingly move to the sides. He threw off his shirt, and holding his breath, ran headlong into the cold water where he stood shivering with the other men. When his feet were numb from the cold, he considered his job done and joined his sleeping wife.

A day or two passed and Harry grew a bit anxious. He hadn't spotted Hannah again and their time in Wellfleet was running out. Tina was growing suspiciously weary of his trips alone and his dull-witted excuses. It was difficult to escape notice in a town this size. Surely, more than one Wellfleet citizen had branded him a pedophile or a stalker already. Some of the happy greetings from earlier in the week had a certain wariness to them now. He also frequented the nearest art supply store more than was normal for a man who didn't know the appropriate name for reddish-brown.

"Not taking advantage of the lovely weather, huh," the clerk had said just this morning. "Tied to your canvasses?"

He'd only a few days left before their return to New York, to their tasteful apartment in the east eighties. He wasn't sure what he wanted from Hannah but couldn't help but pursue it.

On Tuesday morning while Tina was doing her aerobics tape, he parked outside Hannah's house on Pearson Street, hoping he wouldn't run into the daughter again. Was she his? It was difficult guessing her age. She could be eighteen or twenty-five. Would Hannah have kept such a thing from him?

She came out of the house at eight-fifty wearing jeans and an oversized linen shirt. So she hadn't joined the business world or at least not the one he traveled in. Climbing into the Accord in the driveway, Hannah headed toward town, Harry following at a distance. Within minutes, she pulled up to a weathered building on a sandy side street, climbing a rickety flight of stairs on the side. He looked the building over carefully, deciding there must be a studio upstairs where large windows lined two sides. So she'd settled into being an artist. Perhaps her husband's career allowed such a luxury. Or perhaps she was a wildly successful painter, selling canvasses as fast as she could turn them out, yet feeling sadly alone in that house full of children. He tried to see through the windows but they'd been covered with a film to prevent this.

Now what? He couldn't sit here all day, and this stalking was going to get him into trouble. Why not get it over with? Knock at the door and see what happened. He thought it over for a minute or two more, then climbed the stairs. It was possible she might be happy to see him, glad to relive old times.

"Yes?" she said, opening the door. Looking at him more closely, she said, "Oh for God's sake, it's Harry." When he didn't immediately respond, she added, "Well, isn't it?"

He nodded. "I saw you the other night at dinner. I was surprised too." He stepped inside although an invitation hadn't been offered. "Is this your studio?"

She looked around too, as if seeing things for the first time. "What? Oh, no, not mine," she said. "I'm selling this building. I sell properties nowadays. Harry, what the hell are you doing here?"

"On vacation. Got tired of the Long Island beaches."

"No, I mean here. In this studio. How did you find me?"

Not answering her question, he said, "I thought you would've ended up an artist," he said. "Always had a paintbrush in your hand back then."

She fidgeted, not seeming to know what to do with him. "Yes, well..."

"Actually I'm up here looking for a summer place," he said, continuing the lie he'd begun with her daughter. "You were recommended. The name York, you know. It fooled me. I didn't put it together until now." She stared at him, speechless.

"Something small that takes care of itself. The place, I mean." He was babbling. "Do you have anything like that?" Where the hell was all of this coming from, he wondered. Where had he learned such prevarication? On Wall Street, he decided.

A pause. "I mostly handle commercial properties, but I might be able to come up with a few ideas." She relaxed a bit. "Truthfully, Harry, I don't quite know what to say to you. This is a shock." Her mouth tightened. "You took off without any warning twenty-five years ago. Then I received that letter from an attorney. Oh, that was heartless. Ooh, I shouldn't have said that. Forget I said it. I don't want to relive it."

Heartless. This had never occurred to him. It had felt finished to him and he assumed she felt the same. They hadn't spoken for weeks before he left. A bit like now with Tina, actually.

Harry pulled himself together. "But you recovered pretty quickly, right? I saw you with your daughter at the restaurant last night. She looks like you at that age. What is she…twenty-two or so?" He looked around. "Can we sit down for a minute? It's a shock to me too."

She shook her head. "No. So you want to look at some properties, right? Why don't we make an appointment to show you some houses? Maybe tomorrow? Today is kind of busy."

"Sure, we can do that. Shall we meet at your house?" He realized it was a mistake before it was out of his mouth.

"My house?"

His mind went blank. And then. "I happened to spot you coming out the door this morning."

Her eyes could have drilled holes in his forehead. "For Christ's sake. No, you didn't, Harry. I live in a completely unlikely place for you to stumble on. So you tracked me down at my house and then followed me here?"

"Look, can't we sit down? There are some things I need to say to you. Things I have wanted to say for thirty years."

"Say them if you must. But on your feet."

"Hannah, baby, it was a big mistake. Leaving you, I mean." He was almost convinced of it. Almost sure, it had been like that. Almost positive he'd regretted it. Right now, he only knew he had to put his hands on her again. Smell that old smell, feel the lushness of her body. Tina was so hard; there was no give to her flesh. He needed some give. He needed…

And she did go soft then, her body nearly falling onto the stool behind her. Before either of them could take a breath, he'd swept across the room, grabbing her by the shoulders, pulling her in for a kiss, rubbing up against her the way he did years ago. Yes, he could feel her collapsing into him. It was so right. He got hard faster than he thought possible and pushed up against her so she'd know it too. This was going to happen. She started to pull away, but he drew her back in, sealing his body against hers. He was fierce. She must know how much he wanted her. He could feel her heart beating, he could feel…

She screamed. It was a long scream, coming from the depths of her belly. It seemed likely it would never end, in fact, He was surprised the windows hadn't shattered, that his ribs hadn't cracked.

Then Hannah shoved him away so fiercely, he almost fell. The stool toppled over behind them, hitting the floor hard.

"Are you crazy?" she finally spit out. "You dare to put your hands on me? You dare to put your prick on me?"

"I know that look. You wanted it. You always did like to play coy." Or was that Tina?

"The only thing I wanted was for you to leave. I wanted to get away from you as fast as I could."

"But you were willing to meet me tomorrow?" She'd said that, hasn't she?

"I would have sent someone else, you fool. I would've left town rather than run into you again."

"I just thought…Well, never mind what I thought." He was breathless for some reason. "Is she my daughter? Tell me that and I'll leave. I felt some connection."

"What do you mean you felt some connection? With Rachel?"

"Something in her voice."

"When did you speak to Rachel? How dare you speak to her. How dare you say her name aloud. You better not have laid a hand on her. And no, of course, she isn't your daughter. She was born years after we divorced."

"It was outside your house. We exchanged a few words. I never touched her. How could you think that?" He put a hand out, a plea.

She batted it away, and suddenly she had her cell phone in her hand. "How could I…" she spit out. "Rachel, is that you? Are you okay?" She listened for a minute. "Good. Did some man come to the house looking for me?" Hannah looked him over. "An old man, balding, overweight?"

Is that how she saw him or was she being mean? He turned away, afraid of what he'd hear next."

"Looking for who? Oh, okay then. It's someone else. Some potential client. See you in a few. Wait a minute, Rachel, be careful."

She listened a minute and put the phone down. "So you tracked me all the way to Wellfleet? With what in mind, Harry? A final fuck, was that it?"

"It's not like that at all. My wife and I…"

"Your wife!" Now she was laughing hysterically. "You brought your wife along." Sweeping across the room, she picked up an oar propped over the fireplace. "Get out of here now, Harry. Go or I'll take off your head. I'm pretty good with these things, you know.

We've got one or two of our own. Or do you already know that? Of course, you do."

Reflexively, he put his arms up. "I'm sorry it turned out like this."

She laughed. "Rather than a final roll in the hay, right?"

"I never planned…"

"Goodbye, Harry. Go find that nice wife who puts up with you. She must be a keeper."

Back at their rental, Tina's things were gone. The counters were scrubbed clean, the refrigerator emptied. There was no note. No call on the cell he retrieved from the car. Nor a text message. No email.

It wasn't until he went to the bedroom to pull his suitcase from the closet that he noticed the manila envelope on the desk. His name was printed neatly on a label, the name of a law firm on the upper left. There was no printer here. This envelope had been prepared back home. Readied in New York for this trip. Was their vacation in Cape Cod always meant to announce she was leaving? Or had he been given a chance and played things badly again?

Frank Zafiro is one of those writers that will always be something I'm not: a Czechoslovak linguist. He was also in military intelligence and followed that up with a career in law enforcement, so why does he write about bad guys so much? Good question. Anyway, Frank is a very prolific author, writing novels solo as well as having mastered the art of collaboration, working with a number of authors, including Eric Beetner (from issue one) and Jim Wilsky (from later in this issue). Watch for the first in the re-release of their Ania series from Down & Out Books in April, Blood on Blood. *Before you get to the books themselves, we have the first of two prequel stories, the first presented here, for the very first time...*

Adam Raised a Cain
Frank Zafiro

The first time is the toughest, they say. And they float that little nugget of bullshit about everything, don't they? It's always hardest the first time, and then it gets easier and easier. Hell, I don't know. Maybe for some things, that's true. But that hasn't been my experience.

I came on the job with no illusions about cops or the city of Chicago. I grew up in this town, and I know how things work. Most people are struggling to get by and everyone is looking for an angle. A badge doesn't change that nearly as much as it should. What I didn't realize was that for some people, the badge is just another opportunity. Another tool to help you run another kind of game with the same end in mind.

I should have known. My old man, Gar Sawyer, was a career heister. Usually, he was small time, and we lived mostly hand to mouth when I was a kid. But sometimes he scored a good haul, and that made for one or two decent Christmases. Then he left my mother for his Polish mistress, and things went back to being hand to mouth.

Through it all, I saw how he interacted with the cops more than once. See, I didn't have the frame of reference that he was the bad guy and they were the good guys. He was my old man, and until he bailed on me and Ma, he was the ultimate good guy. These cops that were always hassling him and sometimes putting him into cuffs? *They* were the bad guys.

It didn't help that Gar talked shit about the cops at any opportunity, including when they came around. And he fought with them almost every time he got arrested. There's nothing pretty about seeing your old man get gang-piled by three cops. Worse than that, when he was done fighting, it never failed they'd lay a few more shots on top of it all before they hauled him away.

In those days, though, he'd always come back. Sometimes a day later, sometimes a few days, but he always came back. He'd sit in the kitchen, sipping whiskey and smoking his cigarettes with his black eye or busted nose, and he'd tell me how those crooked fuckers took his last twenty dollars out of his pocket on the way to jail. Then he'd laugh and say they probably spent it on some hustler over on West Garfield.

You can see why he was my hero, and why the cops were the bad guys to me.

Later, though, my eyes slowly opened. First Gar took off to live with, and eventually marry, his Polish girlfriend. At least he had the decency to wait on the actual marriage until after my mother died. When she passed, I had to go live with him and his new family. Along with the Polish wife, whom I refused to call my stepmother, I had to deal with Jerzy, Gar's illegitimate son by her. He was close to my age, and it didn't take a math genius to figure out how long Gar had been seeing this other woman on the side.

Slowly I began to see how dead-end his lifestyle really was. How money was never steady, and never enough. If he'd done honest work, we'd have come out ahead. Yeah, the flush times wouldn't have been so flush but the lean times wouldn't have been so lean, either. Expecting Gar to work a straight job was crazy, though, even when the life grinded him down. I saw it all. How the lines in his face hardened and deepened, and how he started to seem less heroic and more desperate.

Jerzy idolized him. Jerzy wanted to be him. Not me. No, by the time I was old enough to move out of the house, I wanted to be the polar opposite of Gar Sawyer. So I joined the cops, and went from being the red-headed step-child of the family to being the black sheep.

Needless to say, no one came to my academy graduation.

Early on, I was lucky not to get assigned anywhere near my old neighborhood. Other guys on the job told me stories of having to arrest people they grew up with or had gone to high school with. The shit Gar and Jerzy were into, I thought my odds were better that I'd be arresting someone with the same last name as me.

I took to the work, though. Knowing the street helps. There's an old adage that a cop is just a criminal who didn't get arrested young and decided to change sides before he got caught, and maybe there's some truth to that, at least in this city. Knowing the rules of the game on the street made it easier to figure out what was what and to make better decisions. It helped knowing who to talk to reasonably and who to just smack upside the head because you knew they weren't ever going to listen.

Pete Harris was the training officer they put with me with for my last rotation. After I passed my final test and he signed off on me, one of the guys on their platoon retired, so they left Harris and me as partners. If I hadn't been so gung ho about the job itself, I might have objected. Harris wasn't flat out lazy, but he wasn't looking to break a sweat, either. If there was an easier way to do something, he knew what it was and that's how we did it.

What did I learn from Pete? His go-to was how to talk a citizen out of filing a report ("I could write this up, but you know nothing is going to happen with this, right?"). But he perfected the drive-by welfare check, too ("Lights are off, no one's home, it's all fine."). When he was my training officer, I kept my mouth shut and did what he said, because that's what was expected and with my family background I was the last rookie who could afford to make waves. Once I was off probation and he trotted out those beauties, I still didn't say anything. I just took out my pen and started the report, or shut off the patrol car and went to knock on the door. Pete would give me a pained expression and shake his head like I just gave twenty bucks to a scam artist or took in a stray kitten, but he'd go along. Not backing up your partner was the biggest sin there was, even if he was making more work for you.

My real education came from Al. He was our sergeant, and looked every bit the Italian Chicago cop. A little jowly, trending toward fat, with a permanent half-day's growth of coarse beard on his face. Al was bigger than life. He not only took care of his men, he did it with the same zealotry of a Marine platoon sergeant at war in the trenches. There was a time I got in a good scrap with a Haitian who'd been selling illegal swag on the street. It wasn't much of a beef but the guy had warrants and he bolted while I was checking his name through dispatch. I chased him for three or four blocks before he turned down a blocked alley. Instead of giving up, he turned and charged at me, snarling.

I gave as good as I got, and by the time Pete caught up to us, we were at a stalemate. Pete tackled the guy from the side, and we got him hooked up. Sarge arrived a few minutes later while I was still dusting off my uniform and inspecting the damage.

"He do that to you?" Sarge asked, pointing to my cheek.

I hadn't looked in a mirror yet, but I could feel a burning, throbbing sensation on my cheekbone, and figured it would bruise up shortly. "Yeah," I said.

"Mother-*fuck*-er," Sarge growled, and then he tuned up the Haitian before we left that alley.

I didn't need him to do that, and some would say it was wrong, but I learned something that day. Sergeant Al Molinari had my back.

Later, on my first trip through Internal Affairs, I was happy for that. There was a bullshit complaint that I smacked a guy around before taking him to jail, then stole his money. His booking photo contradicted his lies about the beating but the money was a he said/he said sort of problem. It was chicken shit, and I didn't do it, but the union rep couldn't seem to be bothered to make time for me even though my dues were paid up. Sarge guided me through it, though. He told me what to say and what not to say and it worked out exactly the way he said it would.

Why am I telling you all of this? Simple. So you'll know why I said yes to him the day he suggested what he did.

That first stretch of time on the job was maybe the best time in my life. I was out from under the shadow of Gar Sawyer, for one thing. By then, he'd taken a fall for robbing a convenience store just over the border in Wisconsin and was doing his time up there. I think Jerzy was also incarcerated around then, but maybe he was out. Either way, I wasn't living in that dark, Polish house any more. I was part of something different, something bigger than myself. Something good. Maybe not perfect, maybe not pure...but *good*.

I lived with that belief for a while. Yeah, I did what needed to be done to take care of business, but even those things I wasn't proud of doing felt like they had a noble purpose. They weren't intended to line my own pockets.

One night, Pete and I went on a domestic dispute. A union plumber who worked long hours finally figured out that some guy down the hall was checking the pipes under his wife's kitchen sink while he was out, so they got into it. By the time we arrived, she had a split lip and he was icing his hand. It wasn't much of an investigation.

Sarge was in the area and swung by when we asked for someone to take pictures of her face. He snapped some photos. All the while she was chirping about how it was all over between them and she was moving before he got out of jail. At the word "jail" he tipped over and suddenly the four of us were in a knock-down brawl in the tiny kitchen, WWF-style.

Unless you're at the home of a gun nut, kitchens are almost always the most dangerous rooms in a house. Lots of knives and other weapons of opportunity come easily to hand. But that night it was dangerous because a two-hundred-forty-pound plumber didn't like the idea of going to jail for giving an unfaithful wife what she had coming to her. The way he saw it, after the beating she got, the two of them were pretty much even.

So we crashed around the small kitchen, grappling with him, bouncing off cupboards and banging against the counters. Eventually I got hold of one wrist and twisted it so hard I was afraid it would break. The plumber screeched in pain and collapsed to his knees. We piled on and got him prone. Pete managed to get the cuffs around his wrists while Sarge knelt across the back of the man's neck, huffing and puffing, sweat streaming down his fat face. He looked at me and tipped me a wink.

"To protect and serve," he muttered with a wry grin.

We got the plumber to his feet. The wife harangued him all the way through the living room and out the door, making sure he knew that she was going to leave his ass as she threw punches while we dragged him out.

Once we reached the street, I stood him next to the patrol car and searched him. He didn't have much in his pockets but his wallet was full of money.

"How much is here?" I asked him, as Sarge walked up. Pete was still upstairs, probably lining up a return trip while the wife's blood was still up. That was one of his things.

"Nine hundred something," said the plumber.

"You always carry that much?" Sarge asked.

"I just cashed my paycheck."

I counted the money out in front of him. "Nine hundred thirty-two. Sound right?"

"Close enough."

"No, not close enough," Sarge said. "Is that right?"

"Yeah. What is this, a fucking bank? Just take me to jail so I can post bond and get to work tomorrow."

"Yeah, sure," said Sarge, and we stuck him in the back seat. Then Sarge grabbed the rest of the plumber's meager possessions, including the wallet. "I'll get Pete. He can ride with me. Meet you at jail."

I drove the poor bastard to jail, resisting the urge to rub my chin where he'd caught me with an elbow. I wasn't even angry any more. After the way I cranked on his wrist, I figured it was a wash.

At jail, we went through the slow, meticulous booking process. I walked him through most of it, then Sarge showed up. "Take off, kid. I'll finish this up."

"Yeah?"

"Yeah. Get back in service. Pete's waiting outside."

No one had to tell me twice. Booking perps was boring work. If Sarge was willing to stand by while the corrections people did their thing, I was happy to let him.

I left the jail, picked up Pete, and we got back at it. Things got busy, and for most of the night we ran from call to call. Finally, around three in the morning, it slowed down and we managed to stop for a break at a diner. Our orders of coffee and eggs had barely arrived when the hulking shadow of Sarge appeared.

A moment later, a pair of white envelopes dropped on the table. There were no markings on either one. Pete reached out and took one of them. He didn't hesitate, scooping eggs onto his fork with one hand while the other hand tucked the envelope into his jacket pocket.

I stared at the remaining envelope. "What's this?" I asked, though I knew, I fucking *knew*, exactly what it was.

Sarge slid into the seat next to Pete, forcing him to push over. "It's your taste."

"Taste of what?"

Sarge cocked his head at me. "You kiddin' me, rook? Don't be a snotnose."

The white envelope stared up at me, malevolent. I wondered if it was from the plumber or if there were other scams Sarge and Pete were running. Either way, I didn't move to pick up the envelope. I just stared down at it. I had a momentary image of the envelope biting my hand as I reached for it.

"Go on, Mick," Sarge said. "You earned it. Hell, you maybe earned yours more than either of us." He pointed at my chin.

So the plumber, then.

"I don't want it," I said quietly.

Pete pretended not to hear me, continuing to shovel eggs into his mouth. My own plate of food sat in front of me, cooling.

Sarge's eyes narrowed. "I didn't ask what you wanted."

"The guy works for a living," I said, looking for a way out. "I don't want to—"

"*That guy* assaulted a cop. Namely, you. So fuck *that guy*."

I thought about it for a second. I glanced around the diner to see who was within earshot. A few people were close enough but none seemed to be listening. "What about her, then? The wife. We should drop the money off—"

"She's a cheating bitch who's leaving him for some dope down the hall," Sarge said easily. "Who she was banging while he was out working. So fuck her, too."

"Sarge, I—"

Sarge leaned forward. "Listen, Mick. You're a good kid. And you're doing good work. Don't mess anything up now."

"I'm not trying to."

"The hell you ain't." He motioned toward the envelope with his head. "This is the way things work. He screwed up. You got yourself hit, for God's sake. This is your compensation."

I shook my head slightly. "It can't be like this," I whispered.

I knew Chicago was a dirty town, and I knew the cops were no different. But not letting some crook give up when you're on the backswing was one thing. Even keeping some of a drug dealer's cash or writing in a report how he never ditched the gun while running away was something I could understand and overlook. In the end, it was all part of putting the bad guys away. But taking money from a working man? For no reason other than we could?

It wasn't right.

Sarge's expression dropped into one of dark rage. He opened his mouth but that was the moment Pete chose to finally speak up. "Jesus, Mick. This is the real world. Grow the fuck up."

Sarge closed his mouth and watched me. So did Pete.

I saw it all then. If I wanted to be part of this fraternity, I needed to follow the rules. And this was one of them, whether I liked it or not. I could try to swim against the tide but at this point in my career, the consequences would come with a reputation, a sort of stink that would follow me around for years.

I took the envelope.

Sarge smiled. "Now that you're a grown-up and all," he said, motioning to the food on the table, "how about you pick up the tab, too?"

I paid for the meal, though most of mine remained uneaten.

The small envelopes appeared intermittently, whenever chance provided opportunity. I started to notice that Sarge showing up on calls wasn't random. He either went to the important ones that required a supervisor, or appeared at the promising ones that might net some bounty or another. Basically, he was either sergeanting or pirating.

I asked Pete about the envelopes one night. He didn't respond right away but gave me the same dark look that Sarge had given me that time at the diner. In the years since, I've come to understand the ingredients of that stare. Mostly it was anger, the kind that is directed at a threat. The kind that sees you as something that might take away something valuable. But underneath that, disguised by the dark aggression, I saw something else.

Shame. And then more anger, directed at me, because I was making him feel that shame.

"What's your malfunction, Sawyer?" he asked. "You some kind of saint?"

"No. I'm just being practical. What happens when one of these mopes complains to Internal Affairs?"

"Those rat fucks don't have time to chase weak ass complaints. They're focused on serious felonies. This is penny ante stuff."

"Still, a single complaint is one thing. A slew of them starts to look like a pattern."

"What, are you a detective now? You polishing your badge to go work in IA?"

I shook my head. "Not a chance. I took this job to arrest bad guys, not cops."

"Yeah, well, you're sounding like one of those slime balls in suits right about now."

"I'm just being careful."

Pete grinned. "You don't have to be careful. You just have to trust the Sarge."

And so I did. I didn't mention it again, and I took my envelopes without a word, just like Pete did. I'd like to say I didn't like it, but the truth was that sometimes I didn't mind so much. When it came from a shithead, the money spent well. If it didn't, I socked it away and waited until some of the stench seemed to come off it.

A man can get used to anything, and I got used to the envelopes. They melted into the fabric of policing, along with the late nights, bad coffee, scratching out reports through sleepy eyes, dealing with victims of all stripes, suspects who ran, suspects who fought, and the ones who had the good sense to just give it up. I got used to the white shirts lording over us, the cars being old and in disrepair, and I got used to the police radio never stopping.

Or maybe I hid amidst the worst of it all. I don't know. Sometimes I think the reason we can be so accepting of hideous things is because we are the best masters at lying to ourselves.

One winter night, Sarge came over the radio, calling our unit number. Even though his voice sounded the same as always, I could tell something was up.

"Go ahead," Pete said into the mike.

"Ten-twenty-five," Sarge said. "Location seven."

He wanted us to meet him at one of our pre-designated spots. He was often coy like this for official business, citing officer safety. If the bad guys knew where we were meeting, he'd said, they'd know where they could get to us. But I knew all of that was just smoke for the real reason.

I pulled into the parking lot and found his sergeant's car. I parked with Pete's passenger window aligned with the Sarge's driver side.

"What's up?" Pete asked.

Sarge grinned. "Payday, kids. You know Esteban Herrera?"

I did. He was a small time neighborhood dealer who was on the verge of graduating to mid-level status. I hadn't seen him on the street in months, and said as much.

"That's because he's been busy," Sarge told us. "Busy expanding, but maybe a little too fast. Garvey and Parkwell popped a corner punk who works for him. He was willing to talk and I took the interview. And guess what? Esteban is meeting his supplier tonight and he's in a Costco kind of mood."

"When do we bust him?" I asked.

Sarge shook his head. "It's not what you're thinking. We take him off for his buy money."

I leaned back in the driver's seat and sighed. This wasn't a goddamn envelope. This was full on robbery.

"Problem, Mick?"

"Yeah," I said. "This isn't like what we've been doing. This is a felony, Sarge." I glanced at Pete. "This isn't penny ante under the table bullshit," I said, hearing the pleading tone in my voice and feeling ashamed. "This shit is way over the line."

Pete looked away, saying nothing.

"You're goddamn right it ain't penny ante," Sarge rumbled. "I'm tired of taking big risks for chump change. We take this score, and we're set for the year. Maybe more. That oughta make you happy, son. Lay off those envelopes for a while."

"It's too dangerous," I argued. "He'll have tons of security."

"At the exchange, sure. But that's at three in the morning. We'll hit him at eleven. Security won't be shit."

"How can you know that?"

Sarge's eyes narrowed. "You think I haven't been watching this little puke since he stepped off his corner?"

"He'll retaliate," I said, making a last ditch effort to derail things.

Sarge laughed. "He's still too small time. And when he doesn't make his buy with the big boys, that's the way he'll stay. We won't have to worry."

I didn't answer. Maybe he had been frustrated with the smaller tastes, or maybe he'd just been trying to make me think so. Either way, it didn't matter. He and Pete were going to do this and since Sarge had already counted me in, I really only had two choices at this point. Walk away and end up face down in Lake Michigan or go along with it. Funny how going to Internal Affairs never really seemed like an option. I could probably thank Gar Sawyer for that.

"How's it going to work?" I finally asked.

"Simple. You're going home sick."

"Me?"

"Yeah, you. You're going to be our plainclothes man. Pete and I will back you up in uniform, but we can't just waltz up to him looking like police. We need the element of surprise."

"Where?"

"He's in a warehouse loft, above a TV repair shop on Pontiac."

"Jesus, who fixes TVs anymore," I muttered.

"Who cares? The shop is closed for the night, anyway. The stairs on the side lead up to the apartment. Herrera lives there some of the time, but he works out of it, too. Take out the guy on the entranceway then Pete and I will come in. We'll bust the door down like it's a raid."

"How many guys inside?"

"Maybe one, maybe none. I don't expect Herrera to move to his meeting place until at least an hour before the actual meet. That's where his troops will assemble."

"How do you know all of this?" I asked again.

"Some of it from the corner rat. Some of it from surveillance. You gotta know your neighborhood, kid."

"What about Garvey and Parkwell?"

"Don't worry about them. They think their perp clammed up and swallowed his tongue."

"What are they going to think when they hear about Herrera getting taken off?" I persisted.

"Christ, Mick. You going for Olympic gold in worrying about shit?" Sarge shook his head, turning in his seat and scowling. "They won't think anything, and if they do, I'll take care of them. Okay?"

I'd run out of any objections that would have made sense in the world I was living in. I shut up.

Sarge misunderstood my silence.

"Hey," he called across the squad. "Sawyer."

I looked up.

"If Garvey and Parkwell need the grease, it's out of my end. Now let's do this." He reached down and started his car.

We headed back to the precinct, where I changed into dark street clothes. Once back outside, Sarge gave me a pair of plain handcuffs, a walkie, and a stun gun, as well as a knit cap to top off the outfit.

"I look like a cat burglar," I said.

"Nah," Sarge said. "You look like a guy who doesn't want to get cold when the wind blows in from the lake."

I didn't answer.

They dropped me two blocks from the TV shop and I made my way on foot. Not much was moving this time of night, thanks to the cold. I walked with purpose, my hands thrust deep into my jacket pockets and my head down. I was a picture of a streetwise Chicagoan minding his own business.

I almost missed the place because all the lights were out. I had to double back to the front and search to find the stairs on the side. I wrapped my hand around the grip of the stun gun in my jacket pocket and headed up the stairs.

"Who the fuck are you?" A wiry Hispanic stood by the door, his hands under his armpits, hopping slightly side to side to stay warm. "The shop is closed, man."

"Oh," I said dejectedly. "Do you know when they open again?"

"In the morning, dumb ass. Now get—"

I hit him with the stun gun. He went rigid with a long grunt while the two prongs crackled with the power of fifty thousand volts. When the cycle ended, he collapsed to the ground, disoriented but conscious. I dropped a knee across the back of his neck.

"Make a sound and I'll light you up again," I said.

"*Hijo de puta*," he growled at me, his words distorted by the weight of my body on his neck.

I pulled his hands behind his back and snapped the cuffs into place. Then I pulled out a handkerchief and stuffed it into his mouth.

He tried to clench his teeth at first, but some pressure on his mastoid forced him to open his mouth. Then I rolled him onto his side and into a sitting position. From there, it was easy to kneel behind him and put on a choke hold, just like I'd learned in training. He struggled frantically, but once I got his carotid artery pinched off, he passed out almost at once. I kept the pressure on for a few more seconds before I slowly released him and checked his pulse.

When I let off the choke hold, I undid one of the handcuffs, fed it around the closest support pole that held up the iron stairway, then reattached it to the limp hand. I reached for the walkie, but stopped. Something occurred to me, so I checked through the man's pockets. Sure enough, I came across a key ring. There was no way this guy was locked out here alone on a cold night like this, so one of these keys had to be to the door.

I stood and started carefully trying each key in the door lock. After the third one, the sentry woke up and started grunting and thrashing his legs about. I turned and kicked him in the head, knocking him out cold. Then I went back to work with the key ring.

Two more tries and I had it.

I turned on the walkie and keyed the mike four times in rapid succession. There were three clicks in return. That meant they were on the way.

I should have waited. I often wonder how things would have been different if I had. But thinking about things like that can drive a man crazy. Sometimes it's best to just accept the way things *do* happen. Because I didn't wait. I followed the plan.

Turning the key, I pushed open the door. Spanish rap music played low and the flicker of a TV danced along the far wall. I listened for movement, for voices, but heard neither one. So I slipped inside and made my way slowly toward the living room, keeping as low and into the shadows as I could.

I froze when a familiar shade of blue washed through the windows, flickering and leaping and bathing the entire room. The screaming chirp of tires coming to a stop and the slamming of doors filled the quiet of the night.

"*Qué mierda!?*" shouted someone from the living room.

"*Policia!*" answered another.

Shit, I thought. Pete and Sarge were coming in way too hot.

Then I heard the pounding of feet on the stairs.

Too many feet.

Instinct took over. I ran through the house, needing to find a way out. I threw open two closet doors and one bedroom door before I got to one that led down a flight of stairs to the TV shop below. Meanwhile, right behind me, I could hear shouts of, "Police! Don't move!" and "Show me your hands!" followed by the crack of gunfire.

Herrera wasn't going down without a fight.

I scrambled the rest of the way down the stairs. The door at the bottom was locked so I kicked it in. The store was dark, but I wove my way through the shelves of broken TVs and equipment toward the back of the building. A second door there was locked up like Fort Knox, including a bar with a padlock that lay across the middle. Grayish light poured through a mesh covered window on the same wall. Using my full body weight I was able to grab hold and work the bolts that secured it to the cinder block wall until they came loose. Finally the entire screen ripped free, its jagged edges tearing at my sleeves. The window itself opened easily enough, at least part of the way, and I worked it until I could squeeze enough of my body through and I toppled out onto the ground, grunting as I landed. Without hesitating, I clambered to my feet and ran like hell.

Police cars were all over the neighborhood, and more blue lights filled the night. I flitted from garbage can to stoop to the sides of parked cars, working my way down the street. I was almost out of the neighborhood when I turned into an alley and bumped into a pair of uniforms.

"Where the fuck do you think *you're* going, asshole?"

Time seemed to slow as I stared at their faces. First I thought about taking off but the only way I could go would have been back into the mess I'd just escaped. I considered bullshitting them, claiming to be part of the raid but before I could decide whether that was a good idea or not, the light from the street caught one of them smiling, and I recognized them both.

Garvey and Parkwell.

Son of a bitch. I could have ran. I could have fought. But I had the good sense to give it up.

They took me to a different precinct and let me stew in holding for a long while, only letting me out once to piss. Then the IA suits came in and went to work on me. What was I doing in that alley? Why had I booked off sick? Who else was in on it with me?

I didn't say a word.

Well, that wasn't true. I said one word.

Lawyer.

They pretended not to hear and kept after me. They said I didn't have a right to an attorney, that this was about whether I kept my job or not. Thanks to Sarge, I knew that was bullshit. They were thinking criminal first, civil second. First try to put me in jail, *then* worry about getting me fired.

I told them nothing.

The difference between us was that they both had wives and families to get home to, and I didn't. So I simply waited them out. Finally, the lead sergeant said, "Okay, smart guy. We'll book you, then. Your face will be on the news. You'll make your family proud."

The funny thing was, I thought that might actually be true in Gar's case. And maybe Jerzy's, too. At least my mother wouldn't be around to see it.

When I didn't answer him, the sergeant just shook his head in practiced disgust and left the room. The uniforms took me to jail and booked me. The next day I was back in the interrogation room and we went for round two, and I still gave them nothing.

It wasn't about Sarge or Pete. It was more about how I was raised. Yeah, Gar was a shitty father, but it wasn't just him that raised me. My mother taught me to do the right thing, and the streets showed me what the right thing was. I wasn't a rat.

I'd been inside for a few days when Sarge came to see me. I was surprised, but I supposed he could play the "just checking on my guy" card to avoid suspicion. Either way, he spoke to me with exaggerated formality and spoke in a kind of code that took me a while to figure out. Once I did, though, I gathered what had happened. Not that I hadn't figured it out already. Garvey and Parkwell had either overheard Sarge's interview, or their perp sang some more on the way to jail. Either way, they had gone to the watch commander and he scrambled together a raid. Hell, for all I knew Pete and Sarge took part in it.

That's what really grinded on me. Those three clicks on the walkie. If he'd remained silent, or sent a different signal, I'd have known something was up. So were he and Pete caught by surprise, too? Or had they left me hanging on purpose?

"So you think you might join the choir?" Sarge asked.

I shook my head.

He nodded appreciatively. "I didn't think so. You're a Sawyer, after all."

I thought about that. I'd tried most of my life to be something very different than Gar Sawyer, or that bastard son of his, Jerzy, and yet here I was, in a jail cell, doing exactly what he would have done if he were in the same situation. After all these years, all this time, we were the same. I couldn't stand to think about it.

"It's not that," I told Sarge. "I just don't know how to sing."

In the end, I gave them nothing and they had little more than that. Even the guy that I hit with the stun gun refused to talk. They lifted one of my prints off of his handcuffs, so they had that and the stun gun itself on me but they had no one who would testify. To anything. Herrera hadn't known shit.

Of course, they offered a plea. A bad cop is bad for all cops, so they wanted to keep the whole affair under the radar. They charged me with assault, unlawful detention, burglary, and conspiracy to commit robbery. The plea offer was for me to plead guilty to one count of abuse of authority. I'd resign as a cop and do eleven months in county jail, out in five if I made good time. Once my lawyer realized I wasn't going to consider naming names and taking the stand, he urged me to accept the plea.

"You take this to trial, all they have to do is hit on just one of those counts and you'll get five times as much time than what they're offering here."

"Conspiracy?" I asked. "Really? With who?"

"They've got you in there with a walkie, Mick."

"They don't have shit."

"You're wrong," he said. "They've got the stun gun. They've got your prints on the cuffs. Plus there's a record of you booking off sick then just happening to show up hiding behind some cars two blocks from the crime scene. And who knows how many different cameras you appeared on while on your way to and from the area. How long before the detectives find some security footage with you creeping along that street?"

"It's all circumstantial."

"You want circumstantial? The tread of your shoe might not be an exact match for the scuff on the door that got kicked in, but it will look like one when they show it to a jury."

"Again, circumstantial."

"And circumstantial cases get convictions all the time. You want to leave this up to a jury? Ask a bunch of Chicago jurors how they feel about an accused dirty cop? Think about it, Mick. Think about O.J. and then you tell me it's a good idea."

He was right. I took the deal.

So I did my time. It wasn't all good, either. You're in jail and they find out you used to be a cop, there's trouble. And when someone is coming at you in a small corridor, you don't worry about good time. You worry about survival.

Even so, I was out in eight months. Sometimes I wonder if it was all good time or if they got tired of paying for the cost of sequestering me after the third attack. Whatever the reason, I was glad for it.

I went for a long walk the day they let me out. The failed heist had been in late February, and even though the court wrangling lasted several months, I got credit for time served once the conviction was entered. So by the time I got out, it was almost October and the weather was turning cold again. I made my way through familiar streets until I reached Lakefront Trail. There, the cold wind was blowing off Lake Michigan, cutting through my clothes to bite at my bones. It hurt a little, but it felt clean, too. Sharp. So did the air.

I breathed deep, staring out at the water. Things had to be different, I decided. There wasn't anything left of the life I'd been living before. I had rejected Gar's way, doing what I could to be the opposite sort of man he was, only to find my way back again. My way forward from here had to be a third route, out of the shadow of both Gar Sawyer and the Chicago PD.

I might be my father's son, but I wasn't going to live his life.

For better or worse, I had my own to live.

Author of more than six hundred novels. Co-founder and co-editor (along with Ed Gorman) of Mystery Scene *magazine. Anthologist. Writer of any number of short stories. Editor of nearly three dozen anthologies. Founder of the Private Eye Writers of America (the PWA) and the creator of the Shamus Awards for private eye fiction. Author of numerous series, including several "Rat Pack" novels featuring pit boss Eddie Gianelli. Is there anything I can really say about Bob Randisi other than he really is a true legend? And that I get the privilege of introducing a Danny Bardini "Rat Pack" story here, in our magazine...*

Hey, Hockey Puck
A Danny Bardini Story
Robert J. Randisi

1

"*Who's* out there?" I asked Penny.

She said into the phone again, "Don Rickles is here to see you."

The only reason I'd met so many movie stars and entertainers by 1965 was because of my buddy, Eddie Gianelli. He worked at the Sands, and got in tight with the members of the Rat Pack, specifically Dean Martin and Frank Sinatra. He'd helped them all out of some jams, and because of it became the "go to" guy for entertainers who got into trouble in Las Vegas.

But there were times when he needed my help, and since we've been friends since we were kids in Brooklyn, I helped him. And that meant I got to meet the Rat Pack, Ava Gardner, Marilyn Monroe, Elvis Presley, and more.

But on this particular day in March 1965, Eddie was out of town, which was the reason Penny said, "Don Rickles is here to see you."

"Send him in," I told her.

He came crashing into the room yelling, "Hey, Hockey Puck! Remember me? We met one night when you came to see my act with your buddy Eddie, and the guys. You know, the guys, Frank and Dino."

"I know who you are, Mr. Rickles."

"Naw, naw," Rickles said, "none of that 'Mister' crap. Just call me...'Mr. Warmth.'" He laughed. "Naw, naw, I'm just kiddin' with you. Can I siddown?"

"Sure. Of course, Mis—Don, have a seat. Can I get you anything? Coffee?"

"Naw, I'm good." Suddenly, he was calmer. The "on stage" Rickles had burst into the office, but now he was the "off stage," soft-spoken Rickles. "Look, I got a problem and your guy, Eddie G., he's not in town. But Frank managed to get 'im on the phone for me and he told me to come and see you. So, here I am."

"I'm glad to help, Don," I said. "What's the problem?"

"Some guy's gonna try to kill me," Mr. Warmth said.

"Why?"

"Ah," Rickles said. "I called his wife fat durin' a show. But, hey, that's my act. I insult people. If they come to see me they gotta expect that."

I reminded myself never to go and see Rickles' act with Penny. I had been with Eddie and the guys, last time, and that had made me immune.

"When did this happen?"

"Weeks ago," Rickles said, "and the guy's been stalkin' me and callin' me ever since. And he's a big guy! Look, it's not like I'm scared or anything but...well, yeah, I'm kinda scared."

"What exactly do you want me to do about it?"

"Get 'im off my back! Tell him I was kiddin'. And, if it comes to that, tell 'im we'll pay him off."

"Did it ever occur to you that might be what he's after, a payoff?" I asked. "Has he said anything to you?"

"Not since the first time," Rickles said. "The first time he approached me after a show and said he owed me for insultin' his wife. I didn't think anythin' about it at the time, but then he started showin' up everywhere."

"Do you know his name?"

"No."

"Where he's from?"

"No," Rickles said, "but I'm guessin' he's local since he manages to get to every show."

"Excuse me for askin', but haven't you been stalked like this before, by other disgruntled audience members?"

"Never like this," Rickles said. "The guy is intense, and I'm due to shoot a couple of TV guest shorts in the next few weeks—*Gomer Pyle*, *Andy Griffith*, *The Beverly Hillbillies*. That stuff could lead to my own show and I don't need this guy lousin' that up for me."

"What's the guy look like?"

"You can't miss 'im," Rickles said. "He looks like a weightlifter, and his wife is a Mamie Van Doren wannabe. Hair so blonde it's almost white, and tits out to here."

"Have you seen the wife again since that night?"

"No," he said, "he always shows up alone."

"When's your next show?"

"Tonight. I'm at the Sahara."

"Can you get me a ticket?"

He reached into his jacket pocket. "Got one right here." Handed it across the desk to me.

"You were pretty sure I'd say yes," I said.

"Eddie told me not to worry, that you'd handle this."

"Did he tell you I'd charge a fee?"

"Whatever you want," Rickles said. "Name it."

"No," I said, "this one's on me, since Eddie sent you. Don't worry, I'll find the guy if he's there tonight, and I'll convince him the error of his ways."

He slapped his palm down on his side of the desk.

"That's what I wanted to hear! You tell this hockey puck to take a joke."

He stood up, but didn't leave.

"Must be interestin' bein' a private eye."

"I do meet all kinds of people," I told him.

"I'll bet you do," he said. "Lemme know what happens."

"You'll be the first to know, Don."

"Pretty girl in the outer office," Rickles commented. "Don't bring her to the show. I'm not responsible for the things I say and do on stage. I'm a totally different person."

He left my office and I could hear him in the outer room, once again becoming the on-stage Don Rickles and performing for Penny.

She came right in and asked, "What was that about?"

"Mr. Warmth is afraid somebody's out to get 'im," I said.

"It's no wonder," she said, shaking her head. "I just don't understand his brand of humor."

"Then I guess it's good I've only got one ticket for his show tonight."

"You can have it," she said. "Enjoy."

2

Don Rickles was a riot on stage.

From the moment he came out he was insulting people—and they were loving it. They doubled over from laughter, and I have to admit that my own sides started to hurt just watching from the back.

I stayed there so I was out of sight, in the shadows, and kept my eyes open for the guy Rickles had described. I didn't intend to brace him then and there, I wanted to follow him home.

When I spotted him he was kind of doing what I was doing, staying out of sight. I caught one glimpse of his face while Rickles was doing his act, and if looks could kill, Rickles would have died on the spot. I could see what Rickles meant when he said the guy was intense. Just standing there he looked like he was vibrating, and his weight lifter muscles were bunched. This guy *hated* Don Rickles. I was going to keep a close eye on him, and if it looked like he was finally going to make good on his threats, I'd be ready to do something.

Luckily, on this occasion all he did was stare. Maybe there were too many people around to suit him. In any case, after Rickles' second encore, the guy turned and left the room, and I followed.

Rickles was playing the lounge where Louis Prima and Keely Smith used to play before they got their divorce. The Sahara was a legend on the strip because everyone from Frank and Dean to Marlene Dietrich and Lena Horne had played there. When The Beatles played the Convention Center in '64, they stayed at the Sahara Hotel.

I followed the big guy.

He walked past the Don the Beachcomber Restaurant, named for Don Webber, who bought the Sahara back in '62. Then he cut through the casino which was alive with the triumphant shouts and the defeated groans of gamblers from all over the world. The clanging racket from bells and coin trays of the slot machines followed us as we went out a back door to the rear parking lot.

My car was in the front. There was no way I was going to be able to follow him, so I decided to brace him there. At the same time, I'd be able to get his license plate number.

As he reached his late model Ford and started to put his key in the door lock, I yelled, "Hey, dummy!"

He turned quickly. He was square-jawed, dark-haired and broad-shouldered, straining the seams of a sports jacket and T-shirt. He looked to be in his late thirties, and was decidedly Italian in appearance, right down to the pinky ring. I wondered if he was connected.

"Don Rickles sent me," I said, showing him the gun on my hip.

"What for?" he asked. "To shoot me in cold blood?"

"No," I said, "just to give you a warning. Stay away from his shows, and from him."

The man grinned. "He shoulda thought of that before he called my *cumare* fat." He pronounced it the way most Brooklyn dagos pronounced it—"goo-mada."

"So that's what this is all about?" I asked. "Your big grudge against Rickles is that he called your old lady fat? *Is* she fat?"

"Don't call her my 'old lady!'" he snapped. "She's young and beautiful."

"Then what's the problem?" I asked. "Him calling her fat or me referring to her as your 'old lady' don't change any of that."

"Look," the big *mamaluke* said, "Gina's a sensitive girl. He hurt her feelings, embarrassed her. For that he's gotta pay."

"With his life?"

He looked disgusted. "Nah, I ain't gonna kill 'im. Just take a piece of 'im."

"And when is that gonna happen?" I asked.

"Any time now."

"Well, it's not," I said. "Not any time, sooner or later. *Capeesh?*"

"Ay, you're Italian?" he asked.

"That's right."

"Then you should know ya gotta pay for disrespect."

"The guy's a comedian. That's his act."

"Then he oughta change it. I'm takin' a piece, and that's that."

"You're gonna have to go through me to do it."

That did it. He stretched his neck, shrugged his shoulders, even thumbed his nose; all the clichés.

"Now?" he asked. "Without that gun?"

"Now, later, whatever," I said, "but with this gun."

He looked hurt, wounded.

"I can't fight you if you got a gun," he whined.

"Well, you've got those guns," I said indicating his biceps. "I'm not an idiot. I'm pretty handy with my hands, but you're a big guy. I'm not gonna give you a chance to fuck me up. I'd just have to shoot you."

He pushed his jaw out at me.

"You better watch out, then," he said. "And tell Rickles I'll be back."

He hesitated, as if waiting for me to shoot him, then unlocked his car door, got in, and backed out. As he pulled away I took out my notebook and wrote down his license plate number.

My Italian was extremely limited to what I used to hear my aunts say in the kitchen when I was a kid, but this guy had all the earmarks of a *testa di cazzo*.

Dickhead.

3

I had a contact at motor vehicles run the plate for me. The car was registered to a Ricky Medici, who lived at an address in East Las Vegas. I decided to go out and have a look the next day, just to see who I was dealing with.

I was sitting in my car down the street from his house when he came out, got into his car, pulled out of the driveway, and drove off. A girl had come to the door and seen him off with a kiss. From where I was sitting I could see there wasn't any blonde hair, red lipstick or Mamie Van Doren boobs. This woman had black hair, and was slender and pale. If the Van Doren wannabe was his *cumare*—

his girlfriend—then this had to be the wife. I decided to go in for a closer look.

I drove up to the house and stopped right in front. I decided to play the part of an insurance salesman, just to get a look inside and maybe collect some information on Ricky.

The house was a ranch style with a carefully manicured front yard of sand and stone and picket fence. I went up the front walk to the door and rang the bell. She opened it almost immediately.

"Did you forget—Oh, I'm sorry. I thought it was my husband coming back."

"No, ma'am, just me," I said, with a big smile.

"And who are you?" She cocked her hip and looked me up and down. She appeared to be about thirty-five, was well put together with lots of black hair and hoop earrings. Her tight top and pedal pushers showed off a taut, trim figure.

"My name's Sam Bennett, with Las Vegas Life. Do you have all your insurance needs covered?"

"Well, I don't know," she said. "My husband takes care of that stuff."

"Then could I come in and talk to you about it?" I said. "I might be able to educate you."

She continued to look me up and down, then said, "You might, at that. Sure, come on in, Sam."

I had to slide close by her as she held the door open for me. She smelled good. Up close there were some crow's feet, but they didn't do much harm. I wondered how much younger Ricky's girlfriend was.

"Can I get you somethin'?" she asked, as we entered the living room. "Coffee, juice...a martini?"

"It's a little early for a martini," I said. "No, I'm good."

"You don't have any pamphlets, I see," she said.

"No," I told her. "I don't bother people with all that until I've explained everything. If you're interested, I can go out to the car and get some."

She put her hands on her hips. "What if what I'm interested in ain't out in the car?"

I hadn't noticed it so much in Ricky, but the accent was more pronounced in this lady.

"Ma'am, you wouldn't happen to be from Brooklyn, would you?"

Her eyes widened. "Born and bred. You, too?"

"Canarsie."

"Bay Ridge!" she said. "Wow, I ain't met nobody here from Brooklyn!"

"How long have you lived here?"

"A few months."

"Is your husband from there, too?"

"Yeah, but you couldn't tell to listen to him talk. He hides his Brooklyn accent. So do you."

"I don't hide it," I said. "I've just been out here a long time."

"Well, whataya know?" she said. "A fellow Brooklynite out here in the desert. Now come on, that's worth a drink, ain't it?"

"Well okay," I said. "I'll have some orange juice."

"You just sit right there on the sofa, honey, I'll be right back."

She sashayed off to the kitchen, putting a little extra "sass" into it. I had the feeling she was a neglected and flirtatious housewife, but I had no idea how far she would go.

I found out.

"Whew!" she said, later while we were lying naked in the bed she shared with her husband. "That was somethin'."

"It sure was," I said. "And I blame the vodka you put in my orange juice, doll."

"Aw, honey," she said, "that was just a little pick-me-up."

"And it worked."

This wasn't something I did a lot. I mean, in my business you meet a lot of flirty women, and sure, I flirt back, but ending up in bed with a married woman wasn't something I did often—or ever, for that matter.

When she leaned into me and kissed me while handing me the drink I found the move irresistible, for some reason. It was only when she assured me that her husband was gone for the day that I finally gave in. We disrobed on the sofa, started there, and moved to the bedroom.

She had a good body, with firm little tits and no fat anywhere. There wasn't much tennis in Vegas, and she didn't seem the golf type, so I figured she either worked out at home, or went to a gym.

"We never did get around to talkin' insurance, did we?" I asked.

"Honey," she said, "I really wasn't interested. And please don't get the wrong idea about this. I mean, I love my husband, but he's been a little distant lately, and you coulda been the mailman, I was so horny."

"I'll try not to let that hurt my feelin's."

"Aw, come on, now," she said. "A door-to-door insurance salesman? You probably come across lonely housewives all the time. This ain't the first time you ended up in bed with one."

"Well, no," I said, just to agree with her. "But a lot of them don't love their husbands, they're just stuck in a bad marriage."

"Well, not me," she said. "We only been married two years, and Ricky's on his way up in his business. He's just concentratin' real hard on that, and I gotta understand, you know?"

"Ricky," I said.

"Yeah, Ricky Medici. Oh jeez, I ain't even told you my name. It's Carlotta."

"Carlotta Medici?" I asked. "That sounds...artistic."

"Yeah, don't it?" she asked. "My maiden name was Carlotta Balducci. Not so artistic, huh?"

"Balducci?" I asked.

"You recognize it?"

The Balducci Family was one of the Mafia families that had run Brooklyn for a long time.

"I do," I said. "I grew up with fellas who went on to become Balducci soldiers."

"But not you?"

"No, not me." My buddy Eddie G.'s older brother—who was my best friend—had been killed in a gang war, and that instantly changed the direction of my life. It changed Eddie's trajectory, too. He eventually made the move to Vegas, and when he told me how good it was for him, I did, too.

Now Eddie worked in the Sands, which was mob run, but that didn't make him a mobster. He worked in the casino, not in any of the other mob-run businesses. It was as close to being a Mafia foot soldier as he was ever going to get.

"Well, it sounds like you're a very understanding wife."

"And you gotta be understandin' too, Sam," she said. "This can't happen again."

"I get it, Carlotta, doll," I promised. "No insurance, and no more sex."

She smiled and kissed me. "You're a real sweetheart!"

We got dressed and she walked me to the front door.

"You know," I said, "you never told me what business Ricky was in."

"Trash," she said. "Pickin' it up and gettin' rid of it—but he's in management."

"I see."

"Well, toodle-loo, lover," she said. "It's been fun."

"It sure has," I said.

"Good luck with your insurance," she said. "Try Mrs. Peters, right across the street. You won't get laid, but you might get a sale."

"Thanks, Carlotta."

She closed the door and I walked down the path to my car, got in and sat there. Thanks to "Mr. Warmth," I was now involved with the Balducci family.

4

I couldn't look Penny in the eye when I got back to the office. Penny and I had an on again-off again relationship. She had been my secretary for a long time, though, and I didn't ever want to ruin that, and at the moment we were off. But that didn't mean I wanted her to know what I'd done.

"Mr. Warmth called," she said. "He saw you at his show last night, as well as the 'hockey puck.' He wants to know what you're doing."

"And you told him…"

"That you'd let him know when you had something to report."

"Thanks, Penny."

"Sure."

I went into my office and sat at my desk. I had a bottle of cologne in one drawer, so I took it out and splashed some on, in case Penny got close enough to smell me. Then I sat back and tried to decide what to do.

Ricky Medici was mobbed up. If I tried to take him on, he'd have help. But I couldn't let him hurt Don Rickles. For one thing, Eddie G. would never forgive me. For another, neither would I. But maybe I could reason with the stalker.

I was about to leave when Penny buzzed me.

"Yeah?"

"Danny, it's Eddie G."

"Okay, put him through."

"Hey, Danny? How's it hangin'?"

"Pretty good. Where are you?"

"St. Louis," he said. "I'm here with the guys. They're performing at a charity banquet for Dismas House. Dino asked me to come along."

"Are they all there?"

"All but Joey. He couldn't make it. They got Johnny Carson to sub for him. The show's tonight. But I wanted to check in with you and see if you heard from Don Rickles."

"I did, and I'm tryin' to help him, but..."

"But what?"

"There's a complication." I told him about Ricky being with the Balducci Family.

"Man, that takes me back to Brooklyn. They've got a trash business in Vegas, right? Not a casino?"

"You're right," I said. "They probably pick up the garbage from all the big houses."

"Why not just convince the guy that hurting Rickles will hurt their business," he suggested, "and the Balduccis wouldn't like that."

"You know," I said to him, "sometimes you're smarter than I remember. I've been lookin' for an angle, and I think you just gave me one."

"I aim to please. Say hi to Penny for me."

"Will do. And thanks, Eddie."

"No, thank you, Danny. You're doing me a favor by helping Rickles."

I hung up, and grabbed the Yellow Pages. The Balducci family sure as hell wouldn't have their name on the trash business, but maybe I could pick the right one out. I chose the three biggest companies, but I didn't want to take the time to go to each one, so I decided to try another way.

I buzzed Penny.

"Yeah, Danny?"

"Do you know any of the girls at the Sands?" I asked. "I mean the office girls, not the waitresses or showgirls."

"One," she said. "She's in accounting."

"I need you to find out who picks up their trash."

"She'd probably ask Jack Entratter's girl. I don't know her because there's been a revolving door in that job since—well, you know. The murder."

Entratter had the same girl working with him for years, but a while back she'd been killed. Since then he hadn't been able to keep one.

"Okay, whatever you have to do, get me the information."

"Gotcha."

I hung up, sat back in my chair. I didn't have any other cases, and there wasn't much for me to do until Penny got back to me.

I put my feet up and dozed.

5

When Penny buzzed me I jerked awake, took a moment to look at my watch. I'd been asleep at my desk for half an hour, long enough to earn a crick in my neck.

"Yeah?" I said into the receiver, when she buzzed me again.

"Were you sleeping?"

"What? Sleeping? No! Whataya got for me?"

"Romeo."

"What?"

"You wanted the name of the company that picks up the garbage at the Sands, and…seven other casinos. Romeo Trash Company."

"And are they owned by the Balducci family?"

"Yes."

"According to?"

"Jack Entratter."

"Jack Entratter's girl?"

"No, Jack Entratter himself," she said. "I called my friend, and she didn't know. She put me on the phone with Entratter's girl, but she's too new to know. So I called Jack Entratter himself."

"Really?"

"Why not?"

"Huh. I don't think I would've done that."

"Well, he was only too happy to answer my question, when I told him who I was and who I worked for."

"You mentioned my name?"

"Of course!"

"I didn't think he liked me," I said.

She didn't comment.

"Penny?"

"Anything else, boss?"

"I assume you've got the address?"

"Written down out here, along with the names of the management people. Your Ricky is one of them."

"Okay, I'll pick it up on my way out."

"Where are you going?"

"To check out Romeo."

"What do I tell Mr. Rickles if he calls again?"

"Tell him I'm working."

Romeo's garage and offices were on Paradise Road. From their parking lot I could see the strip in the distance.

I walked through an open garage door, saw a stairway that I assumed led up to offices. Two or three guys in coveralls stood off to one side, studying me. I walked over to them.

"Can you gents tell me where I can find Ricky Medici?"

"Yeah," one said, "he's upstairs in the office."

"Thanks."

"You, uh, here to cause him some trouble?" one of the others asked.

"No," I said, "just the opposite."

"Oh," he said. "Too bad."

"You want him to have some trouble?"

"As much as he can handle," the third guy said.

"Why's that?"

"He used to be one of us," the first guy said, "but since he got kicked upstairs, he turned into a dick."

"How did he manage to get kicked upstairs?"

"He married into the family," the man said. "Got fast-tracked right to the top after only a few weeks on the street."

"And turned into a dick, huh?"

"Ah," the first guy said, "he was kind of a dick right from the beginning."

"Okay, thanks."

"Watch out for Gina," the first guy said.

"His secretary," one of the others said. "She's real...protective."

They all smirked.

"Thanks for the warnin'."

I walked back across the garage and up the metal staircase to the second level. As I passed several windows to get to the office door I looked in and saw a big-boobed platinum blonde Van Doren lookalike sitting at a desk. Ricky's *cumare* was his secretary.

As I entered she looked up at me with big, bright blue eyes.

"Yes?"

"I'd like to see Ricky."

"Are you a cop?"

"Why would you ask me that?"

"You look like a cop."

"Is there some reason why the cops would be here?" I asked.

"There's never a reason why cops come around, but they come around," she said.

"Well then, no, I'm not a cop."

"So who are you?"

"Danny Bardini," I said. "I'm a private detective."

"What's a private eye want with Ricky?"

The guys downstairs were right. She was protective.

I decided to tell the truth.

"You guys went to see Don Rickles one night, and Mr. Rickles made some comments that upset you."

"That's right," Gina said. "He was an ass."

"Well, that's his job, doll, to be an abrasive ass on stage. But Ricky threatened him, and keeps on threatenin' him. I'm here to make it stop."

"You ain't gonna make Ricky stop doin' anythin' he wants to do." She wasn't the sharpest knife in the drawer, but she was no dummy.

"Well, I guess I'll just give it a whirl, sweetie," I said. "I'm sure the Balduccis aren't gonna want one of their employees getting into a mud-slinging war with a friend of Frank Sinatra's."

"Oh!" she said, blinking. "I—I never thought of it that way.

Maybe you better go in."

"Do you wanna buzz him?"

"That's not necessary." She pointed to the door behind her.

"Thanks." I walked past her, through a cloud of her perfume.

I opened the door, entered, saw the empty desk, and the feet sticking out from behind it. Ricky lying on the floor behind the desk, dead as yesterday. His head had been bashed, and there was a pool of blood.

When I went back out to the reception area, Gina was gone.

Who's the dummy now, I thought.

6

"So you think the broad had somethin' to do with fingerin' him?" Detective Hargrove said to me.

"Why else would she keep me out there talking, and then just let me waltz in without buzzing him first?"

"Because she knew he was dead."

"Right."

Hargrove didn't hate me as much as he hated my buddy, Eddie G., but it was a close race. Still, when I called in the murder I knew he'd show up.

He said, "Oh, it's you," as he walked in. Then he took a look at the body behind the desk.

"Your work?" he asked.

"I found him this way."

He asked what I was doing there, and I saw no reason not to tell him the truth. Then I filled him in about Gina.

"All right," he said, "we'll have to find her. The employment department here'll have her address." He looked at his partner, who I didn't recognize. He was always getting new ones.

"I'll take care of it," the partner said.

"Anything else you wanna add?" he asked me.

I didn't want to steer him to the wife, where he might find out that I'd had sex with her. Besides, what'd she have to do with this? If she wanted to kill him, she could do it at home. So I said no.

"I wonder how the Balduccis will react to this?" Hargrove said.

"Beats me," I said. "I was wonderin' what they'd think about him gettin' into it with Rickles, a friend of Frank Sinatra's."

"We'll talk to whoever runs this operation in Vegas," Hargrove said. "No reason to get involved with the Balduccis in Brooklyn."

"Good idea."

Then he looked at me and asked, "You still here? If I need you, I'll call you."

And that was it. I was dismissed, which suited me.

I went back to the office to call Rickles and tell him his problems were over.

I didn't know mine were just beginning.

7

I called Don Rickles from my office and he invited me up to his suite at the Sahara. He said he was trapped there doing some interviews and couldn't get away, and he'd appreciate it if I came over.

As I got there a man was on his way out and let me in. He was a dour looking man with sad eyes who I recognized right away. He introduced himself as Don's friend, "Bob."

"Don's finishing up an interview, Mr. Bardini," he told me. "If you'll just wait?"

"Sure."

"I have to go," he added. "My wife's waiting in our suite. We'll be going out to dinner with Don and Barbara."

"Oh, is his wife here?" I asked.

"No, she and my wife went shopping. We'll all be meeting when he's finished here—or after you and he are done."

"I won't hold him long," I promised.

"Thanks. We'd appreciate that." He turned and yelled, "See you later, Don!"

"Soon, Bobby!" Rickles shouted.

I went further into the suite, saw Rickles sitting on the sofa. In front of him was a man with a microphone and a recorder.

"Are we done?" Rickles said to the young man, "because you're startin' to bore me. But I kid. In all sincerity, just let me say…your questions are stupid."

The young man laughed and laughed and then they were done. Rickles saw the man out, then turned to me and said, "Ay-yay-yay!

Drink?"

"Sure," I said, "finding dead bodies makes me thirsty. Bourbon."

He went behind the bar and stared at me while he poured the drinks.

"Are you a kidder, Mr. Bardini?"

"Not this time, Mr. Rickles."

"Hey," he said, "it's Don."

"Okay, Don," I said, accepting the glass from him. "You won't have to worry about Ricky Medici anymore."

"Medici? Is that his name?"

"It was," I said. "He's dead."

"Jesus!" he said. "You weren't kiddin', were you?"

"No. I found him lying behind his desk. Somebody'd crushed his skull."

"This have anythin' to do with—"

"No," I said. "I didn't kill him to get him off your back."

"I'm just sayin', that woulda been above the call of duty."

"Yeah, it would've been," I said. "No, fact is, he worked for an outfit owned by the Balducci family."

He paused with his glass halfway to his mouth.

"*Family* family?"

"That's the one."

"Great, I ticked off a guy who's connected."

"Was connected," I said. "That's probably what got him killed, although..."

"Although what?"

"Well," I said, "he had a wife and a girlfriend. The girlfriend worked for him."

"And?"

"And she kept me in the outer office for a while before letting me go inside to find him dead. When I came out, she was gone."

"So you think she set him up for a hit?"

"She either set him up," I said, "or she killed him."

"Well, a crushed skull doesn't sound like a professional hit."

"No, it doesn't." I put the glass down. "Thanks for the drink. I gotta go. If you need anything else, let me know."

"I should be good," Rickles said. "I appreciate the help."

We shook hands and I left his suite.

8

I didn't want to tell Detective Hargrove what I was thinking. If he wasn't smart enough to think that she may have been more than just the finger, that was his problem.

I didn't have an address for her, and I knew Hargrove and his partner wouldn't share. But I did have one address, and maybe she'd be able to tell me something helpful. After all, she was a Balducci.

I drove back to Ricky Medici's home, hoping to find his wife still there. Maybe she'd been notified about his death, and maybe not. If she had, I'd be the bearer of sad tidings. If not, I'd be a shoulder to cry on.

I rang the doorbell and Carlotta answered.

"Well, well, the salesman," she said. "Back for another round? I told you it was a one-time thing, but it's flatterin' that you came back—and we still got some time before my husband comes home—"

"Carlotta," I said, "I'm not a salesman."

"You don't think I knew that?" she asked. "You're a cop."

"Not a cop," I said. "Can I come in for a minute? I've got some bad news for you."

"Sure, why not?" she said, and backed away. Just inside the door she asked, "What's the bad news?"

"Ricky's dead," I said. I couldn't think of any other way to say it, or soft soap it.

"How?"

"Somebody clubbed him to death in his office."

She stared at me for a few seconds. "You want a beer?"

"Sure."

I followed her to the living room, where she waved me to a chair. She went into the kitchen, came back with two cans of Piels. Then she sat across from me on the sofa.

"I told him workin' for my family would get him killed sooner or later," she said.

"I wonder if that was it, though," I said.

"Why? Who else do you think would wanna kill him?"

"Well," I said, "I met his secretary."

"Gina? Why would Gina want to kill him? She's his *cumara*." She pronounced it the same way Ricky had.

"You knew about her?"

"The poor man's Mamie Van Doren?" she said. "Of course I

did. I ain't stupid. I know I'm married to an Italian man. My father always had a *cumara*, my brothers have 'em, why not my husband?"

"And that was okay with you?"

She blew some air out from between her luscious lips and said, "No. But what was I supposed to do about it? My mother put up with it and was married for over sixty years."

I sipped my beer.

"Aren't you gonna have one when you get married?"

"No," I said. "My wife will be the only woman in my life, if and when that happens."

She made that noise again, then stared at me. "You mean that, don'tcha?"

"I do."

"But you've got a girlfriend now, and you fucked me this mornin'."

"I'm not married," was all I said.

She drank some beer. "Okay, so why are you here, if it ain't for a fuck?"

"I wanted to see what you thought about who might've killed him," I said.

"Why do you ask?"

"I found him," I said. "I guess I feel like I might've saved him if I'd gotten into his office earlier."

"Why didn't you?"

"Because Gina was holdin' me up outside. Then she let me through without buzzin' him first."

"That's unusual," she said. "That broad wouldn't let *me* go into his office without buzzin' him first."

And there it was, the reason I had come. Just tumblin' from her mouth without her knowin' it.

"Okay," I said. "Thanks for the beer, and I'm sorry about your husband."

"Where ya goin'?"

"To see if I can find Gina," I said. "The cops have her address, but I don't. I guess I could get it from the office."

"Or," she said, "you could get it from me."

9

I drove to the address Carlotta gave me. It was just off the strip and looked like a hot sheet motel, complete with women showing their wares in bikinis at the pool. Later, after dark, they'd be showing those same wares on the streets in short skirts and halter tops.

I doubted that if Gina had fingered her boss/boyfriend that she would have come back home, but figured there might be something in her room that could help.

Carlotta said she was in room 8, which overlooked the pool. I was going to have to be careful that no one saw me forcing the door.

As it turned out, I needn't have worried. The door was not only unlocked, but ajar.

I knew better. I should have turned and left, but I went in.

It was a simple motel room, with a king-sized bed, table, chairs, dresser and television in a corner. It had been tossed, so there were women's clothes all over the room, including a bra hanging on a lamp shade. In the center of the bed lay Gina, not naked, but lying in a very immodest pose. Her skirt was up over her hips, and her panties were gone. She obviously wasn't a natural blonde. Her top had been torn so that her enhanced breasts were exposed. I didn't touch her, but when I walked around the bed I could see her head was bloody. She'd been killed the same way her boyfriend had, with something heavy.

I decided this time I wasn't going to call the police from the scene and wait. I left the door as I had found it, slightly ajar, wiped my prints from the knob, and made my way back to my car, hoping to attract as little attention as possible. Since the girls around the pool weren't working, but relaxing, they paid me little to no mind.

I got in my car and drove until I found a phone booth away from the motel and out of plain sight. I called the police, left an anonymous tip and then drove on to my office.

10

When Hargrove showed up the following day it was no surprise. As usual, there was distaste in Penny's tone when she buzzed to tell me he was at her desk. He typically made some ugly remarks to her he thought were flattering, which went a long way toward explaining why he'd never been married.

He entered my office with his partner in tow.

"Where'd you go yesterday after you left the scene of the crime, Bardini?" he asked.

"Good mornin' to you, too, Detectives. I assume you meant Medici's murder? I came back here and did some paperwork. Oh, but first I went to see Mrs. Medici."

"Yeah, she told us," Hargrove said. "You beat us there."

"I thought she deserved to hear it from someone who cared about her feelings," I said.

"And how did you happen to know her?"

"While working for Mr. Rickles, I went to the house. Ricky wasn't there, but she was. We talked."

"Talked?" Hargrove asked. "That's all you did?"

"That's it."

I doubted Carlotta had flirted with either of these men. Hargrove was just rude, and his partner was a homely bastard.

"So you didn't go to the secretary's home? Gina..." He looked at his partner.

"...Danza."

"Yeah, her," Hargrove said.

"Nope. Why?"

I waited for him to tell me somebody saw me there.

"She's dead, too," Hargrove said. "Looks like when she left you at the plant, she went home and somebody killed her the same way as her boyfriend."

"Jesus, that's too bad," I said. "She was a pretty girl."

"You should've seen her," Hargrove said. "They left her totally exposed."

"Was she raped?" I asked.

"Not according to the M.E. She was just...posed," the partner said.

"Never mind that," Hargrove told him. To me he said, "You talk to Rickles?"

"Yeah, I told him he had no problem anymore."

"We're gonna have to interview him."

"Why?" I asked. "You can't possibly think he did it."

"He's got motive."

"He came to me to solve his problem."

"So you've got motive."

"Maybe for killin' Ricky, but not the girl. What about the workers there? They didn't like him. They told me so."

"We're lookin' into everybody," Hargrove assured me. "Includeing you, so don't leave town."

"I hadn't intended to."

He looked at his partner. "We might as well head for the Sahara."

"Want me to call ahead and smooth the way for you?" I asked.

"We don't need you for that," Hargrove said. "We have badges."

As if a badge would get him in everywhere.

"Well, good luck with the case," I said. "It's all over for me now."

He didn't bother to thank me, but left my office, made himself feel good by tossing off another remark to Penny about her legs, and left.

She came into the office on those lovely gams and shivered. "He always gives me the chills—in a bad way."

"I know."

"What did he want?"

"They found another body," I said. "The guy's secretary."

"The girl who took off on you? But didn't you think she was involved?"

"I still do," I said. "In fact, I was actually starting to think maybe she killed him, but now...somebody killed her, just like Medici."

"How terrible. So who do they suspect?"

"Everybody," I said, "including Don Rickles...and me."

"Well," she said, "I know you didn't do it. By the way, will we be getting a check from Mr. Rickles?"

"No, I told him there'd be no charge."

"Okay."

"What?"

"I was kinda hoping we'd be able to pay the rent this week," she said. "The landlord called."

"That's okay," I said. "I'll call him. But *you'll* be gettin' paid. Don't worry."

"Oh, Danny," she said, "you know I never worry about that."

She turned and walked out.

I sat back in my chair, replayed everything I'd been thinking about during my night of no sleep. It all boiled down to who had the best, and most personal, motive to kill Ricky. No matter how many ways I thought about it, I kept coming up with the same name.

11

After some phone calls and a drive, I showed up on Carlotta Medici's doorstep for a third time.

"Now you're pushin' it," she said, although tempered with a smile. "I'm in mourning right now."

"Are you?"

She looked at the glass she was holding in her hand.

"Yes," she said. "We all have our own ways of mourning."

"Well, let me come in for a minute and maybe I can help you make yours a little easier."

She hesitated, then said, "I'm gonna let you in because I've been a little lonely, thinkin' that Ricky won't be comin' home."

She turned and walked into the house. I entered, closed the door and followed. I found her in the living room, holding her drink, standing in the middle of the room. She was wearing a sleeveless T-shirt, a tight pair of pedal pushers, and no shoes. I remembered tickling those toes with my tongue, then pushed the thought from my mind. Unfortunately, I couldn't push away the sight of her hard nipples making themselves noticed from beneath her top.

"By the way, I know the police came by. Thanks for not rattin' me out for—well, you know."

"Fuckin' me?" she asked, wriggling the glass so that the ice clinked. "I didn't want them to know, either. Besides, that one guy was a real prick. And he doesn't like you."

"I know that."

"Oh, I'm sorry. Drink?"

"No thanks."

"Coffee."

"No."

"Well, I think I know what you might want, but you'll have to come back another day—"

"No," I said. "I don't want that, either. In fact, you should know that I never do that."

"Then I'm flattered," she said. "You broke a rule for me."

"It's not a rule, it's just not somethin' that happens a lot."

"I'm sure you come across a lot of grieving widows, or just lonely housewives, in your business, don't you?"

"Well, yeah, but I don't offer that service."

"Maybe you should," she said. "You're real good at it, and it might help make some of them feel better. I know it made me feel somethin'."

We'd gotten off the track. In fact, we'd never gotten onto it.

12

"Gina's dead, Carlotta," I told her. "Somebody killed her in her motel room."

"Too bad."

"She was killed the same way Ricky was."

She sipped her drink.

"I gotta say, you really don't seem to be mourning all that much."

"Well," she said, "I gotta admit it'll be nice not to have anybody calling me 'Carly' anymore. I hate that name."

She clinked the ice in her glass again, then walked over to a small portable bar on wheels and poured some more gin into her glass. That was it, gin and ice.

"Why are you here...Sam?"

"My name's Danny Bardini," I said. "And I'm here because I think you killed your husband and his *cumare*."

"I see," she said. "Can you prove it?"

"No."

"Are you recording this somehow?"

"I wish I'd thought of that."

"Hold your arms out."

She put her drink down and frisked me with great attention to my crotch, which responded in the way she expected.

"I remember you," she said, caressing me through my pants.

"You mind?"

She laughed, went back and picked up her drink.

"Okay, yeah, I killed both of them."

"Why?"

"I got tired of the situation," she said. "As you know, I like sex. Ricky liked it, too…with Gina. He said he was thinking of leaving me for her. I couldn't allow that."

"Well, that's a motive to kill *her*," I said, "but you killed him, first."

"I went to the office to talk to her, but somehow Ricky figured out what I was gonna do. He took me into his office, started to shout and threaten me."

"I don't get it," I said. "You're a Balducci. Didn't that matter to him?"

"Apparently Gina's obvious charms were enough to make it not matter. Or he figured the success of the business would keep him safe."

"But not from you."

"No," she said. "He was sittin' at his desk, tellin' me how it was gonna be. Him and Gina, with me on the outs. I couldn't have that. I pretended to be upset, and when he turned around to get me some water, I picked up a paperweight from his desk and hit him with it. It killed him. At least it did eventually."

"And then you left?"

"No," she said. "First Gina came in and caught me."

"Why didn't you kill her then?"

"What Ricky didn't know," she said, "is that Gina and I were also…involved."

"You got to Gina before he did?"

She shook her head. "It wasn't like that. See, Daddy didn't like the way Ricky was livin' his life. He told me I better get my husband in line. So…I hired Gina."

"You what?"

"I hired her to keep Ricky busy by becoming his *cumara*. We went to the same gym. I knew she needed money and the work, and I figured if Ricky was busy with Gina, he'd stop doin' the other shit that was botherin' Daddy—mainly gamblin'."

"So that's why she let you get away and kept me in the outer office as long as she could."

"Yeah."

"Then she left and met you at her motel?"
"Right."
"But you killed her."
"Well, yeah. I did."
"Why?"
"You want a drink?" she asked.
"Yeah, I think I need one."

She poured two more drinks, handed me one. I couldn't understand why Ricky cheated on her. Carlotta was sexy as hell. But then I've never understood the male desire for "strange."

"Why did you kill her?" I asked. Again.

She smiled. "Poor little Gina got greedy. She said she thought it might be nice bein' married to Ricky, and I ruined it. She thought a little payoff was necessary. Actually, she was thinking more like a big payoff."

"She tried to blackmail you."

She nodded. "If I didn't pay she was goin' to the cops. After all, all she'd done was sleep with a married man. I told her that wasn't gonna happen. We argued, she kept threatening. I still had the paperweight in my purse, so I took it out and when she turned her back, I hit her."

"Why did you pose her after? In such a humiliating position?"

"I thought it would confuse the detectives," she said. "Maybe they'd think an old boyfriend did it. Besides, she was kind of a slut."

"Well," I said, "they were confused, but that's sort of Detective Hargrove's normal condition."

"How did you figure out it was me?" she asked.

"I didn't, not really," I said. "In the case of a husband bein' killed the logical first suspect is the wife. And with his girlfriend also bein' killed...well, I just thought I'd ask."

"Why not think one of the goons he worked with did it, or somebody from a rival family?"

"They would've used a gun."

"Ricky has a gun in the house," she said. "I almost took it with me."

"Now that would've confused the detectives, for sure."

"It still might." She brought her hand around from behind her back and pointed a .32 automatic at me.

"I hate to do this to you, Danny," she said, "but you're the only one who knows."

"So why bother telling me if you knew you'd have to kill me?" I asked.

"I guess I just needed to see how much you knew, and how much you told the cops."

"I don't get along with the police, so you're safe there."

"That's good to hear."

"But I don't think you're gonna be able to pull that trigger, doll."

"Why not?" she asked. "You know I already killed two people."

"Yeah, but that was with a paperweight," I said, "which I guess is around here somewhere."

She didn't respond.

"It's a little harder with a gun."

"Is it?" She pulled the trigger, and nothing happened. I darted forward and ripped the automatic out of her hand.

"Especially when the safety's still on."

In this month's column, Jeff Pierce gives us a little something different. Rather than share his unique insights into the world of the near-off soon-to-be released, he turns his perceptive insights into one of the best crime writers ever to write short fiction, Stanley Ellin. Haven't read him? Fame garnered from shorter works may be even more difficult to sustain but as Jeff reminds us, Ellin was also a gifted if not prolific novelist. An essay on Ellin's longer works is long overdue, as is an Ellin revival in general. I can't think of a better place to start...

Placed in Evidence
Non-Fiction
J. Kingston Pierce

As unjust as this might be, Stanley Ellin isn't usually thought of as having contributed greatly to the twentieth-century development of private-eye fiction. When he's remembered at all nowadays, it is for his award-winning short stories, most of which debuted in *Ellery Queen's Mystery Magazine* (*EQMM*), and some of which were adapted as episodes of TV suspense series such as *Alfred Hitchcock Presents*, *Ghost Story*, and *Tales of the Unexpected*. But then, it was as a short-story writer that Ellin initially made his mark.

Born in the working-class Bath Beach district of Brooklyn, New York, in 1916, Stanley Bernard Ellin went on to graduate from Brooklyn College at age nineteen, try his hand at such occupations as steelworker, dairy farm manager, and teacher, and be discharged in 1945 from wartime service with the U.S. Army. Shortly after leaving college, he'd married a former classmate named Jeanne Michael, who established herself as a freelance editor (and, he said, "a brilliant, remorseless, and objective critic."). It was apparently she who convinced her literature-loving spouse to become a full-time fictionist— a decision that may have seemed rather imprudent at the outset.

71

Indeed, Ellin's first story, "The Specialty of the House" (about a restaurant boasting a sinister signature dish), was rejected multiple times before *EQMM* finally published it in 1948. However, that abbreviated yarn—now considered a crime-fiction classic—led to dozens of others, and eventually helped earn him prominence. "No short-story writer ever achieves actual perfection," observes the blog of America's Short Mystery Fiction Society, "but no short-story writer ever tried harder to achieve it than Stanley Ellin. And few came closer."

Although Ellin won a couple of Edgar Allan Poe Awards from the Mystery Writers of America for his short fiction, it wasn't solely in that field he excelled. Over the course of his forty-year career, he produced more than a dozen novels. They ranged from his 1948 revenge tale, *Dreadful Summit*, to 1972's *Mirror, Mirror on the Wall* (a work about sex, macho self-hatred, and violence that British author H.R.F. Keating included in his 1987 list of the 100 best crime and mystery books), to 1985's *Very Old Money*, focusing on out-of-work schoolteachers who join the servant staff of an affluent family that can't seem to dust the skeletons from its closets.

In addition, Ellin concocted four gumshoe narratives, each impressive in its own way, and at least the first two of them meriting mention among the last century's most distinctive such works.

Being a perfectionist, Stanley Ellin didn't embark on composing *The Eighth Circle* (1958), his first and best-recalled book starring a private investigator, without preparation. "Ellin studied several PI agencies before writing the novel," explains Kevin Burton Smith of *The Thrilling Detective Web Site*, "so *The Eighth Circle* is a far more authentic look at real PI work than most PI novels." His labors were rewarded: *The Eighth Circle* captured the 1959 Edgar Award for Best Mystery Novel.

This yarn introduces us to Murray Kirk, the thirty-something son of a Gotham grocer. He used to be a lawyer, but not too successfully, so he applied for a job with Frank Conmy's upscale Manhattan firm of confidential inquiry operatives, and was engaged on the spot. The work turned out to be better than clerking in a law office, but it didn't quite fit his preconceptions of life at a detective agency. Early on in the novel, Kirk remarks to Conmy's prim secretary, "It's not much like the movies, is it?" To which she responds: "No, it isn't, Mr. Kirk. We don't supply booze, blondes, or bullets. As a matter of fact, no one here is licensed to carry firearms except Mr. Conmy himself, and I very much doubt if Mr. Conmy knows one end of a gun from the other."

A decade after joining Conmy's firm, the founder has passed away, leaving the business—and his pricey apartment over-looking Central Park—in Kirk's care. Everything seems to be going well for Ellin's protagonist until he's presented with the case of Arnold Lundeen, a vice squad cop caught up in an extensive corruption scandal linked to a city-wide betting ring. Lundeen's idealistic lawyer comes to Kirk for help, and he makes a decent case for why Kirk can do some good for the accused policeman. But what ultimately secures this high-living sleuth's involvement in the matter is Lundeen's fiancée, schoolteacher Ruth Vincent, an ebony-tressed, long-lashed lovely ("it was incredible that a cop, a dumb, dishonest New York cop, should ever have come into possession of anything like this."). It doesn't take long for Kirk to grow more interested in being with Ruth than he is in keeping her boyfriend free of the slammer. In fact, Kirk reasons that if he could somehow reveal Lundeen's guilt without leaving behind evidence of that perfidy, Ruth might be more vulnerable to his own wooing.

In many respects, Murray Kirk is the archetypal Ellin peeper. He's clever and successful, well-connected and far from world-weary, with big-city swagger and expensive tastes. He demonstrates few of the self-sacrificing and noble motives common to so many of his fictional ilk, but instead possesses "a businessman's sense of ruthlessness and priorities," as Robert A. Baker and Michel T. Nietzel put it in their 1985 survey of American detective fiction, *Private Eyes: One Hundred and One Knights*. The trouble for Kirk in *The Eighth Circle* is that his professionalism gets in the way of his selfishness. Thanks to the example of Frank Conmy, he's turned into a fine detective and even a fine man, despite his self-doubts. The more Kirk tries to direct the case to his benefit (something that isn't lost on his veteran employees), the more he learns to respect—even envy—Lundeen's attorney, and the clearer he recognizes his cop client's innocence. How, then, can he go through with his scheme to live with Ruth and still live with himself?

Far from endeavoring to "transcend the genre," this character-propelled book sought to enrich it, to give it a broader, if less heroic scope. "The crime-fiction genre offers the writer infinite diversity of theme and treatment," Ellin is quoted as having said. "I like to take advantage of that diversity." With *The Eighth Circle*—one of my favorite private-eye novels of all time—he certainly fulfilled that goal.

Twelve years and half a dozen books later, Ellin returned to PI fiction with *The Bind* (1970). Set in Miami Beach, Florida (where the author had a second home), its lead role goes to Jake Dekker, a former Manhattan newspaper reporter turned freelance insurance investigator. Dekker's selfish and calculating streak is even less well concealed than Kirk's.

The plot finds Dekker hired by New York-based Guaranty Life Insurance Company to determine whether the recent demise of a middle-aged policy holder, Walter Thoren, can be blamed on an accidental car wreck (in which case Thoren's widow collects a double-indemnity payment of $200,000) or was the consequence of suicide. The cops found no mechanical problems with the automobile and no intoxicants in Thoren's system. Dekker, though, has evidence that Thoren, who grew rich heading up his late father-in-law's photo-processing outfit before retiring, had experienced money troubles over the last two years, and he believes Thoren may have been the target of a blackmail scheme. If he can prove the man died by his own hand, and convince his widow to drop her suit for payment, Dekker will collect $100,000.

He enlists in his undercover plan a shapely blonde, loquacious part-time actress Elinor Majeski—a naïve twenty-one years old to his thirty-five—and the two of them masquerade as husband and wife at a rental property next door to the Thorens' home, situated in an exclusive (read "no Jews") community outside Miami Beach. Elinor gets busy modeling bikinis in hopes of drawing information from Thoren's concupiscent son. At the same time, Dekker plants bugs on nearby phones and seduces (for a worthy cause, of course) a lustful Latina neighbor who is convinced Thoren was murdered for having sided with saboteurs intent on toppling Cuba's Fidel Castro. With the case becoming ever more convoluted and dangerous, Dekker turns for additional assistance to an aged but honest shamus named Abe Magnes, who better understands the local ropes and players.

Thoren's widow flees as this storyline twists; mobsters and Everglades yokels enter the picture, and suspicions are raised that Thoren's premature passing may link somehow to intrigues dating back to World War II. Despite her conviction that Dekker is cold-blooded and singularly money-driven, Elinor starts to develop romantic feelings toward him—which only heightens the tale's tensions as she's attacked during an ocean swim and later endangered by flying bullets. It doesn't take a genius to see that Dekker made a mistake bringing her into this game and that he was right when he cautioned Elinor not to weigh her needs against those of his doing his job ("You're in for a terrible disillusionment if you do.").

The atmosphere of Ellin's story turns progressively more ominous, and its conclusion, though satisfying, is shocking. So Hollywood's decision to convert *The Bind* into a 1979 comedy-romance picture titled *Sunburn* must have made the novelist's eyes roll all the way to the back of his neck. Farrah Fawcett, then at the height of her jiggle-glam fame after starring in *Charlie's Angels*, was cast as a distinctly vapid Elinor opposite deadpan comic actor Charles Grodin as Dekker, with the great Art Carney wasted in the Magnes role. Filmmaker/critic Peter Hanson opines in his blog, *Every '70s Movie*, that *Sunburn* is "neither amusing nor seductive," and "bombard[s] the audience with stupid attempts at bedroom farce and high-stakes action." You're better off skipping the flick and finding the book.

Baker and Nietzel note in *Private Eyes* that Ellin's snoops-for-hire are typically motivated to take on an investigation by "an obsession with a woman for whom the case becomes the way by which her love can be captured." That was true in *The Eighth Circle*, and it's equally accurate when appraising Ellin's final two gumshoe novels, *Star Light, Star Bright* (1979) and *The Dark Fantastic* (1983).

Both are headlined by John Anthony Milano, whose "Johnny" nickname seems at odds with his cultured demeanor and—as with Murray Kirk—his urbane preferences in clothes, champagnes, girlfriends, and office décor. Like his creator, Milano grew up in Bath Beach, and his mother and "hotshot lawyer" of an elder sister still live in Brooklyn. Milano, on the other hand, has done his best to shed any hint of humble roots. He has a ritzy apartment in a Central Park South co-op, drives a Mercedes-Benz, and—after years spent handling security and detective responsibilities for "fancy hotels"—is a full partner in Watrous Associates, a Madison Avenue private investigations agency.

Unlike Ellin's previous PI outings, *Star Light, Star Bright* is a first-person account, with narrator Milano being summoned to Miami by Sharon Bauer, a former film celebrity of German-Mexican descent, who Milano rescued from trouble in London three years ago. The pair thereafter became lovers...until the younger Sharon ditched Milano at the behest of Walter Kondracki, a con man and "astrologer to the stars," who insisted she instead wed Andrew Quist, a wealthy but arthritic philanthropist decades her senior. Now, Sharon needs Milano's aid again. She'll pay $20,000 for him to head off a homicide at the expansive Quist estate, the designated target—a resident there and a recipient of several threatening missives—being the aforementioned Kondracki, who has restyled himself as pontifical mystic Kalos Daskalos.

What we have in these pages is basically an Agatha Christie-style country-house whodunit, with the eccentric suspects including several "movie people" (all hoping to fund their latest project from Quist's deep pockets) and Maggie Riley, a plucky art historian and Jack the Ripper expert, serving as Quist's confidential secretary. A convenient blackout, Milano's amorous attentions toward Maggie as well as Sharon, and our sleuth's perfunctory efforts to protect the spurious sage all keep the plot moving swiftly. Yet in the end, *Star Light, Star Bright* is an often humorous mystery more ordinary than innovative. Had Milano not been cast in its sequel, he might well have slipped into obscurity.

"Controversial" is the term most often applied to Ellin's *The Dark Fantastic*. Due to the corrosively bigoted views expressed by its chief antagonist, that psychological suspense yarn was rejected not only by the author's longtime editor at Random House, but also by "several other publishers," recalls Otto Penzler, a prolific editor of crime-fiction anthologies and the proprietor of Manhattan's Mysterious Bookshop. Penzler, who in 1975 had established a small publishing house called The Mysterious Press, eventually came to Ellin's rescue. "I read [*The Dark Fantastic*] and thought it was a brilliant work," he tells me, "and offered to publish it. It got an amazing, two full-column review in *The Wall Street Journal*, among many other good reviews. I was (and am) proud to have published this very good book by a very good writer and a very good man."

The story follows two overlapping plotlines. In the first, we have Johnny Milano, annoyed at having just turned forty, trying to locate a couple of pricey pre-Impressionist paintings stolen from a private California collection. The collector's insurance company figures those beachscapes are "on their way to a middleman working out of New York." Milano, who apparently developed a keen knowledge of art while coming up in the world, suspects the intermediary is jet-setting but shady Wim Rammaert, owner of a gallery near Carnegie Hall, so he reconnoiters that showroom, sniffing for clues. In the process, our not-quite-a-hero develops a pulse-racing interest in Christine Bailey, Rammaert's headstrong, twenty-three-year-old African-American receptionist. Trying to get closer to her, Milano proposes that he pay Christine to help him nail Rammaert; but she wants his professional expertise rather than his lucre or lust. It seems she has a pretty mid-teens sister, Lorena, who's recently acquired clothes with cash from an unknown source, and Christine wants assurance that those funds aren't ill-gotten.

Here's where the second plotline comes in. It involves that earlier-referenced bigot, one Charles Witter Kirwan. He's a widowed, sixty-eight-year-old retired history professor, and he lives in his grandfather's elegant Queen Anne-style Brooklyn home, right next door to a degenerating 1920s apartment building he also owns, constructed by a subsequent Kirwan progenitor. Throughout his teaching career, Kirwan had endorsed his liberal colleagues' support of Gotham's large black population. But after being told he has lung cancer and not long to live, he's decided to strike back against the blacks (he calls them "Bulangas") who Kirwan blames for despoiling the neighborhood his Dutch-rooted family helped found. With more than seventy sticks of dynamite at his disposal, Kirwan intends to raze his four-story apartment structure, killing himself and most of his renters. Those occupants include Lorena Bailey, who lives there with her mother and brothers.

What makes this novel difficult to read, is that Ellin alternates third-person chapters about Milano—whose pursuit of Lorena's secrets leads him to discover Kirwan's catastrophic scheme—with others told in first-person from the ex-educator's perspective. The author obviously abhors Kirwan's opinions, but is also fascinated by his character's psychological and moral collapse. For Ellin to place himself inside the mind of that cadaverous racist over and over again confirms his commitment to expanding the detective genre's "diversity of theme and treatment," but it must have left him rattled after each day's writing.

One can't help but wonder whether, having sent Johnny Milano out on two assignments, Stanley Ellin thought him durable enough for a third adventure, or more. "As far as I know," says Penzler, "Stan had no plans to do another Militano book, but then Stan almost never talked about his books or stories in progress."

Sadly, Ellin penned only one more novel before dying, at age sixty-nine, in 1986.

"It's like the wildest of the men's adventure novels of the '70s, updated for the new millennium. Definitely not for the faint of heart."

—Bill Crider, author of the Sheriff Dan Rhodes Series

Globe-spanning Barry Lancet, this issue's feature writer, weaves us a tale of his series' character Jim Brodie: private investigator, antiques investigator, and adopted son of Japan. Barry's first book in the series, Japantown, *won the Barry Award, he's been a finalist for the Shamus Award, and the latest entry in the Brodie series,* The Spy Across the Table, *is soon to be out in paperback.* Japantown *has been optioned by J.J. Abrams and Warner Brothers so the character of Brodie may be the next big book-to-big-screen hero we see from the world of crime fiction. What I love about "Three-Star Sushi" is the chase scene Barry gives us, that sort of "espionage" novel we get as we follow Brodie on his track to solve the mystery in...*

Three-Star Sushi
A Jim Brodie Story
Barry Lancet

Less than six hours after sitting down to some of the best sushi in Tokyo I found myself surrounded by a pumpkin-headed American sumo wrestler and a yakuza enforcer out for blood. All for a case I never wanted and for a client I was sure wasn't telling me everything. But it's the kind of situation you could find yourself in if you turned over the wrong rock in Japan.

Especially when your luck bottoms out.

The day began when Ken Sato invited me to his restaurant for lunch, dangling his famous culinary masterwork as bait. He offered a second place setting for Jenny, my ten-year-old daughter, and I accepted for both of us. Given my family history with Chef Sato, I could hardly refuse.

But I was suspicious, so I wanted Jenny along for insurance.

Proximity no doubt played a role in Sato's invitation. Sushi Sho was not far from Brodie Security, the PI and security firm established by my father some forty years ago, a big stake in which he left me when he died. Sato had been one of my father's first clients, and later, a friend.

The master chef practiced his art in a discreet shop tucked away down a tangle of cobblestone backstreets in an upscale section of the Japanese capital. The tangle had been born some time in the seventeenth or eighteenth century when Tokyo was called Edo and ruled by a shogun and an elite group of samurai. Back then the enclave had been a knot of dark and drafty wooden hovels. Cooks and maids and bottom-rung samurai lived in them and catered to the whims of the ruling class residing in more luminous quarters higher up the hill.

I parted the short blue entry curtain and slid the wooden door aside. Jenny, a fireball of energy, wiggled in ahead of me and ran up to the counter calling Sato's name.

"Welcome back," the celebrated chef said in Japanese, his eyes tracking my daughter's progress with apparent fondness. He was short and puffy and had cheeks flush from a lifetime of eating with purpose. But the cheeriness ended there. The rest of him was pale and sagging, like a loaf of bread pulled too soon from the oven.

"It's good to be back," I said in the same language.

Eight well-dressed customers sat at the sushi bar. Each had waited six months for a sitting at Sushi Sho, with its three-star Michelin rating, the highest rank handed out by the company's *Red Guide*. I wondered who had been bumped to fit us in. We took our places at the end closest to Sato, on tall stools with woven-reed seats. Jenny's black pigtails flapped happily as she clambered up onto the high perch.

The prominent chef turned russet brown eyes on my daughter. "Nice to see you again, Jenny. Your mother was a beautiful lady and you look more and more like her every time I see you, though I can see some of your father and grandfather peeking through."

Jenny had my high nose and natural watchfulness but her mother's gentle brown eyes rather than my lighter blue-grays, and her complexion favored a buttery almond to my pearly white.

"Daddy says that about mommy, too," my daughter said. She

looked down and smiled as she ran her hands over the silky surface of the unvarnished pine counter. "This feels good and I *love* sushi and I'm really really hungry."

Sato chuckled. "I'll take care of you, don't you worry."

Hearing his cue, an apprentice set small porcelain plates in front of us, while behind the counter Sato scooped up a portion of vinegared rice, pressed it into a petite block, laid a rectangle of fresh white sea bream on top, patted the fish lightly, then set the finished sushi in front of Jenny, and the next moment its twin in front of me.

After the bream came red-fleshed yellowtail, then a juicy disc of raw scallop. Then creamy marigold orange sea urchin inside a paper-thin wall of speckled black seaweed. Each offering was set before us like a treasure.

Which they were.

Perfect, edible treasures.

And part of the culinary wizard's opening gambit.

A half hour later, the feast began to wind down. While the other guests talked among themselves, coddled in their carafes of hot saké, Sato leaned forward and in a low voice said, "I need Brodie Security's services."

There it was. A textbook example of the Japanese expression *Tada yori, takai mono wa nai*. "There's nothing more expensive than 'free.'"

I gave him a sympathetic look. "I'm not doing field work this trip. Let me call in Noda. He's our top man."

My life and dual occupations had me straddling both sides of the Pacific. Jenny and I lived in San Francisco, where I ran an antiques shop. But I flew to Tokyo at times to handle work related to my father's firm, half of which I'd inherited. But with my daughter in tow, this time vacation was the focus, not the job.

Sato shook his head. "It's got to be you. It's personal."

"You know Jenny and I are here to visit her mother's family."

As a widower, this was one of my many obligations—and my daughter's cue to chime in.

Jenny turned to me. "It's okay, Daddy. If his world is spinning bad, you should help. I don't mind."

I looked down and winced. *Simply insist we are on vacation*, I had told her. Instead, she'd tossed my personal creed into the mix, one I'd streamlined expressly to give her a handle on life in a way her young mind could grasp. It revolved around the idea that the world keeps turning, tossing out the good and the bad without reason, rhyme, or consideration. You aim for the best, prepare for the worst. You deal with what comes your way and move forward. Always forward. And to date it had worked. In ten short years, Jenny had wrestled with the loss of her mother, her own kidnapping no less, and my occasional brush with the brutality of the duties I'd taken over from my father. However, I never envisioned that she would turn my own teachings against me, especially for a few mouthfuls of sushi. Even if it was three-star, Michelin-grade sushi.

Sato's hand rose, his fingers gently cradling his crowning gem—and the bait with which he'd lured us to his shop. It involved aging a tender cut of tuna that ran along the spine of the big fish somewhere north of the belly. The flavoring technique and the specific part of the fish were carefully guarded secrets.

Jenny pounced on the rarefied tuna, her youthful face radiant. Sato placed a second piece in front of me with an apologetic smile.

It was an offering I still hoped to sidestep.

Until he said, "It's my daughter, Mia. I need you to find her."

After the last diners had departed, Sato came around the bar with two cups of steaming green tea.

"This means a lot to me, Brodie," he said, sliding onto the stool next to mine. "First your father and now you, the second generation."

"And I'm third," Jenny piped in.

"Yes, you are," Sato said. He cast about for his wife, who came forward, took Jenny by the hand, and led her into the back of the shop.

Sato was referring to my role as a second-generation PI, a position I'd assumed by default when Brodie Security fell into my lap. Four decades ago my father had established the first western-style VIP security and detective agency in Tokyo after mustering out of the U.S. Army, an MP and an officer. His firm catered to Japanese companies expanding overseas in need of bicultural know-how. As a teenager I'd spent afternoons and weekends shoulder to shoulder with the staff. I soaked up every scrap of tradecraft and gossip that came my way. In between I'd attended the local Japanese school, where I learned the language, the culture, and the ways of the people. I took lessons in judo and martial arts from top-ranked teachers who were on a first-name basis with my father. At times I was the only Caucasian face among a sea of Japanese, but even so Japan became something of a second home.

By the time I inherited half of Brodie Security, it employed a staff of twenty-three but ran on a shoestring. Competition had chipped away at the agency's once exclusive domain, and rising wages and expenses gobbled up the rest. My salary amounted to a stipend, barely enough to cover my travel from home to Tokyo, but I kept the place running because many of the employees had families to support. Between the outfit my father built and the antiques store I ran in San Francisco, I managed to pay the bills and, in the rare good month, add to my daughter's college fund.

"I'm sorry to intrude," Sato said, "but this is important."

His ashen lower lip trembling, he filled me in about his daughter's disappearance—what he thought could be a kidnapping, although he'd received no ransom demand as yet. "It might be too early to think about it as that," he confided, "or I might be wrong, so I don't want to involve the police. But I also don't want to take any chances."

Once he finished up, Jenny and his wife emerged from the back room. My daughter skipped over to us carrying a gift box. It was perfectly wrapped in ruby red paper and a white lace bow. A small rectangular card was tucked under the bow. Mrs. Sato shot a nervous look at her husband, who nodded. Relieved, her face crinkled in merriment as Jenny set the package on the counter and read the card, a personal message penned in Mrs. Sato's elegant Japanese script.

When Jenny began pulling at the wrapping, Sato's wife tilted in my direction. "You'll bring our Mia back to us?"

"Yes," I said.

She squeezed my hand.

Sato had supplied only one concrete clue: the name of a known yazuka lieutenant. But it was enough.

Jenny lifted a brightly painted wooden top from the confines of the box and spun it. It wobbled and toppled over.

"Like this, Jenny-chan," Mrs. Sato said, the heavy shadow of her matronly bulk smothering my daughter's small form. With a skilled flick of an index finger and thumb, Mrs. Sato made the top dance. It glided across the counter in little swoops, throwing off a kaleidoscope of color.

"Usually Japanese tops are painted with red and yellow and green stripes," she told Jenny, "but this one is special. It's painted in a rainbow. All us girls should have a rainbow in our lives."

The message was clear: Mrs. Sato wanted her rainbow back.

And below the forced good cheer, her concern told me the Satos' world was spinning bad.

I sat behind my father's old wooden desk in a high-backed leather chair. The leather was brown and soft and webbed from decades of use. Hovering over a laptop, Jenny was playing video chess in the client chair, her black pigtails swaying gently as thought. On the other end of the digital clash was her best friend Lisa, who played from San Francisco, where it was nearly ten-thirty at night.

Without looking up, my daughter said, "Lisa's mom says Lisa's got to go to bed in fifteen minutes. Can you talk to her? We need more time."

A Japanese short sword hung on the back office wall, a souvenir from my father's reign. There was also a first-place certificate for a shooting competition on the LAPD gun range, awarded during his truncated career on the force. My father, like me, didn't take orders well.

"Nope. You can finish tomorrow."

"Daddy, it's only two-thirty here."

The door to the office flew open and Kunio Noda stormed in. Jenny let out a yelp of surprise.

"I'm sure there was a knock in there somewhere," I said.

Noda scowled. "Got him. Let's go."

"Now?"

"Tiger always has breakfast at his favorite ramen shop around four."

Saburo "Tiger" Takagi was the name of the Japanese mafia lieutenant we were chasing. He was middle management for a powerful local yakuza gang. Most yakis were night owls, so their day started late. The nickname suggested a habitual ferocity we were about to put to the test.

I turned to Jenny. "You heard. Mari will take care of you until I'm back."

"Is this about Mia?"

"Yes."

"Okay, then."

"That's my girl."

According to Chef Sato, his daughter's safety was contingent on handing over twenty percent of Sushi Sho.

Unless I could find another solution.

Noda and I sat in a white Nissan Bluebird, staring at Kabochan Ramen Shop from the shadows of an alleyway across the street and four doors down. We were in Komagome, a dusty ramshackle district along the eastern edge of central Tokyo.

"Does a white Bluebird make sense to you?" I asked Noda.

"Take it up with Nissan."

Brodie Security's chief detective was not one for small talk. Or humor. But he was one of our best operatives so everyone put up with his quirks. He was a bulldog in human form. Bulky and broad-shouldered, with an eyebrow severed by a yakuza blade during a skirmish. Noda had more than repaid the slight. Behind the ill humor were quick hands, a keen mind, and eyes that missed nothing.

He said, "You *know* Sato's holding back, right?"

"I do."

"Gang's got a hook in."

"'Cause they don't come after your business unless they have something solid on you. Kidnapping doesn't come down unless there's a reason."

"So what's the hook?"

"Didn't ask."

"Why not?"

"Wasn't the right time."

At a quarter to four, Tiger Takagi turned the corner. He wore an electric blue blazer over a black silk shirt. Muscles rippled under the shirt like rats tunneling through garbage. He had thick lips, a thick nose, and a chiseled look forged from years on the street. It was a ruggedness a certain type of woman went for when seeking adventure. A trip rarely worth the fare.

The yaki disappeared into the ramen shop. Which had yet to open for dinner.

"Special privileges," I said.

Noda grunted. "And smart business."

For whatever reason the owner couldn't refuse Tiger's patronage, so he served the yaki lieutenant before opening to the public.

We waited. And waited. Then a black stretch limousine pulled up to the front of the restaurant.

The sleek car gave me hope.

Stretch limos were for show or sell. Either VIPs were chauffeured or business was conducted. Tiger was middle management. Not a lowly foot soldier but not yet entitled to the perks and privileges of an upper slot, which meant the car was for business.

Which might lead us someplace useful, or nowhere at all.

Tiger pushed open the ramen shop door, wiping his mouth on the back of his hand. He eyed the limo, glanced up and down the street, then slipped into the vehicle.

"Driver didn't get out for him," I said.

"Noticed," Noda said.

The limo eased away from the curb and disappeared around the next corner. Noda swung the Bluebird into the street. Three blocks later he positioned us two cars behind the sleek black machine. We followed it through the backstreets of Komagome and over a glimmering expanse of the Sumida River, Tokyo's main waterway. A pair of fishing trawlers chugged listlessly upriver after having dropped their catch at Tokyo's massive fish market.

Three blocks later we rolled into Ryogoku, and the peaked green roof of the national sumo stadium swung into view.

Noda's cell phone chirped. He answered, listened, said "Be there in twenty," and disconnected.

"You're leaving?" I asked.

"Trouble with the Mitsu-Sumitomo Bank case."

I nodded but said nothing. When trouble surfaced there was no better man to have around. Too bad I'd be losing him.

Noda dipped his head in the direction of the arena. "You go in and see what there is to see."

"That's the plan."

"Public place. Big crowd. Stay away from trouble."

"It's yakuza."

"*Try* to stay away from trouble."

I shrugged.

The limo sidled up to the wrestlers' entrance. A straggle of die-hard fans waited for a bone crusher to emerge. They aimed their cameras at the luxury vehicle with shaded windows, then grew puzzled when a yaki—rather than a sumo wrestler—stepped from the car.

Noda said, "Can't go in the wrestlers' gate."

But Tiger had, which bothered me. "Cruise over to the main entrance."

Tokyo's sumo stadium, the Kokugikan, beckoned from behind an ornate wrought-iron fence. A row of brightly colored banners set on bamboo poles flapped in the light afternoon breeze, each trumpeting a different wrestler's name.

Noda pulled to the curb. I stepped from the car, wished him luck with his problem, then eased up to the nearest booth and asked for a ticket. Behind plate-glass a burly ex-bruiser in his fifties stared at me glumly.

"Sold out," he said.

I was afraid of that. "You sell standing room?"

"No."

"Any last-minute cancelations?"

He snorted. "Four hundred tickets go on sale every morning at nine. Come back tomorrow."

Dead end.

I looked around and caught a discrete huddle at the end of the block. A *dafuya* scalper with a customer. Dafuya were independent small fry who affected a cheesy yakuza look but possessed none of the menace. This one had gone retro: a man's ankle-length faux fur coat in black and a close-cropped punch perm.

I strolled over and asked for a ticket.

"Only got prime seats, *gaijin*. Gonna cost you."

Gaijin meant *foreigner*. Sometimes it was a neutral label, sometimes not. This time it was a bargaining chip I wouldn't allow him to cash.

"Try again," I said.

His glance wavered and I said, "Look, take your mark-up but don't get carried away on me. I know you pick up spares for peanuts."

Corporate ticket holders snapped up the bulk of the prime seating in lots of four and handed them out to customers or employees. Beneficiaries sold off their extras for cash, often at rock-bottom prices.

"I got twentieth row, arena."

I shook my head.

He shrugged. "Suit yourself. Front or back?"

"Front."

I would need the highest level of access, or close to it, to move about without restriction.

"Direction?"

The stadium was divided into quadrants, each designated with a direction of the compass. North and south gave you a side view of the face-off. East and west put you behind one wrestler, with a frontal view of the other. Rabid fans had a preferred viewing angle.

"Any."

"Well, I got prime seats, two boxes back. East. Eye level. Cost ya sixty."

Sixty thousand yen was the equivalent of six hundred bucks.

"What else you got?"

"Fourth box. South. Mid-arena. For fifty thou."

"It cost you ten. I'll give you fifteen."

"I'm not running a charity. You want the rear of the arena level, you can have that for fifteen. Fifty for the box."

"Twenty-five."

"Forty. Only three more days left. If Mitanoumi wins today he could take the championship."

"I'm here for the atmosphere. Thirty."

"Thirty-five. And that's a bargain 'cause you speak the language."

Three hundred and fifty dollars, American. One sitting at Sato's shop ran three hundred. Before drinks.

"Sold," I said.

He grinned and we turned our backs on the stadium guards at the entrance. I gave him three tens and a five, and he passed over the ticket.

"You gonna be betting? I got a friend inside."

"No thanks."

"You change your mind, ask for Mazu from Ibaragi at the East snack bar."

I nodded, headed for the entrance, and showed my ticket to a bulky almost-was at the gate. I angled through one of only three turnstiles, and crossed an open square with the other ticket holders, entering the indoor arena at the far left of the quad.

I made my way through a cluster of fans buzzing around in the hall to the correct aisle, then to my assigned spot. Box seats meant a six-foot square area of tatami matting with four square throw cushions—two in front, two in back—cordoned off by an eight-inch-high polished wooden rail.

All around the festivities had begun. Fans toasted the future success of their favorite wrestler, and businessmen entertained clients. Saké, beer, and whiskey flowed freely.

I took my seat and scanned the arena. On each day of a fifteen-day tournament eleven thousand fans filed into the stadium. It took twenty minutes of careful searching, row by row, quadrant by quadrant, to find Tiger. He was huddled with a man of some stature and his assistant, in the second row on the other side of the ring. The assistant wore an off-the-rack navy blue suit and a maroon tie, his boss a tan Armani suit with a brown-and-yellow paisley ascot.

I worked my way back to the lobby, narrowly escaping a collision with a salaryman loaded down with beer, peanuts, and dried squid. I circled around to the north side of the hall and headed back into the seating area. Retrieving my cell phone from my pocket, I activated the photo app. When the next two sumo behemoths in the ring charged, I snapped a picture. Just as the shutter clicked a passerby jostled me.

The flash emitted a surprisingly bright light. The three men stopped talking and Ascot glanced around suspiciously before plunging back into the huddle. I hadn't recognized him but he looked familiar.

I checked the shot. Blurred.

In the ring the next pair of loin-clothed goliaths began the opening rites. Scattered applause greeted their arrival. The noise level rose as the grapplers eyed each other with open hostility and performed their salt-throwing ritual, an offering to the gods said to purify the ring.

For my second attempt at a photo, I worked my way to a spot within four yards.

The two contestants threw more salt, stretched, stomped, and glared. Shouts of support erupted around the stadium, coalescing to an impassioned roar as the sumo faced off for the final time before their charge. Tiger and his box mates suspended conversation and turned their attention to the bout.

On the referee's signal the men rammed each other at center ring and traded wicked slaps to the face. The smaller wrestler—at a mere three hundred pounds—sidestepped a sudden lunge with unexpected agility, throwing his opponent momentarily off balance. Swiftly, the fleet-footed bruiser's hand snaked out for the belt of his larger adversary's loin-cloth and secured a hold. The two struggled briefly, but the smaller sumo weathered the bigger man's attempts to break his grip. Then, with a twisting movement that caused his biceps and pectorals to balloon, the shorter wrestler wrenched the belt up and over, toppling his massive foe to the sand.

All of this and only ten seconds had elapsed.

As the chorus of cheers and catcalls reached its peak, I'd squeezed off the second shot. I was too close this time, so I set up the photograph as a selfie, supposedly framing myself and the ring in the picture. But once more the flash was too bright and the angle was noticeably off, so my ploy crumbled at first glance. But I'd captured the image I needed.

At what turned out to be a very high cost.

The three men turned in unison and stared. Ascot scowled in a way far more unpleasant than anything I'd seen over the last few minutes, and sent Tiger after me.

I barreled toward the lobby, hoping to dash out the way I'd entered. But the number of last-minute arrivals had grown. If I tried to leave by the front entrance, Tiger would corner me in the three-turnstile bottleneck at the ticket gate. I'd have to lose him inside the stadium.

I glanced over my shoulder and noticed Tiger had collected a second yaki who was bigger, meatier, and meaner. He looked like a natural-born brawler, with scarring down one side of his neck.

Off to the left a door reared up. Bold red Japanese characters splashed across it read NO ENTRANCE.

I entered. Fast.

Ten hurried paces brought me to a staircase that plunged downward into darkness. I cast about for another way. There was none.

The doorknob behind me began to turn.

I scrambled down the staircase. The steps were steep and narrow, the stairway seemingly endless. At the bottom I found myself in a long unlit hall. It ended in a set of swing doors. A sliver of light seeped out under the doors. There were no security guards in sight, but the other side of the doors might tell another story.

Overhead I heard footfalls start down the stairs.

I headed for the light.

When I pushed open the doors, bright beams blinded me. Blinking rapidly, my eyes refocused, revealing a maze of wall-less dressing rooms. Each makeshift space was actually a platform of two tatami mats raised eight inches off the ground and separated by tiled pathways three feet wide. Hulking sumo wrestlers and their attendants could trod easily between platforms and leave their footwear below before stepping up onto the elevated mats.

I'd found the back way into the grooming station.

Wrestlers sat everywhere on the platforms, proud and upright. Their eyes were closed. Their legs were crossed. Their massive arms were folded over equally massive chests. Each sumo lorded over his area while behind him an attendant fussed with his hair, oiling and combing and shaping the final topknot for the pending fight.

This was the legendary pre-bout grooming process. It took half an hour to lubricate and shape a sumo's long black locks in the traditional style for a skirmish that finished in seconds. The fighters were expected to endure the tedious procedure with the stoic patience of the warrior spirit they represented.

I eased past the first grouping with a few casual nods. There were no security guards. I was halfway through the second when a voice behind me boomed: "Akeshi, stop that idiot." *Akeshi* was short for *Akeshiyama*, the wrestling name of a popular newcomer.

To my rear Tiger and his friend stood in the doorway. In front of me a mountain of youthful flesh in a wrestler's traditional robe moved into my path. I tried to step around the big lug but he shifted with me. I wasn't going to get past him without a fight.

There was a rustling of bodies to the rear and Akeshi said, "Kenoyama, stay out of this."

In accented Japanese with a bluegrass lilt, I heard a foreign voice ask why.

Kenoyama, a promising American sumo entrant from Kentucky,

had stepped forward. A champion collegiate wrestler back in the States, his prowess on the sumo circuit was such that he had already made headlines in Japan. He was a large-headed youth with orangish-red hair, a disarming Southern grin, and soft pink skin that had caused first-time adversaries in his college days to underestimate him, much to their detriment. After his first televised sumo matchup, none of his Japanese opponents made that mistake.

"His friend supports our beya," Akeshi said.

Meaning Tiger's boss contributed funds to Akeshi's sumo stable. Which explained why Tiger entered through the wrestlers' gate.

The yaki lieutenant grinned at Kentucky but the Southerner shook off the call to retreat. "No can do."

The next instant he grabbed Tiger's bulky partner and slammed him against the wall. The yaki foot soldier smacked his head hard and fell to the ground in a heap, as still as a slab of yellowtail on Sato's cutting board.

"I told you—" Akeshi began.

Kentucky held up a huge paw. "I'm done here. Just figured I'd make it one on one, is all. That's how we do it back home." He gave me a curt nod and I returned the gesture.

No one spoke. The tension rose. With twenty professional fighters and their attendants looking on, the silence pressed in on us.

Tiger glared and called to his friend, who hadn't stirred. "Kaz, get over here."

Hearing his name, the fallen yaki groaned. His eyelids fluttered open, then shut.

Tiger snorted in disgust, his glance darting around the room.

I focused on my opponent while keeping an eye on his sumo watchdog. Nothing guaranteed the big bruiser wouldn't jump into the fray, but for the moment I had to contend with Tiger's compact muscled bulk and upper body strength against my height and reach. Tiger was heavy-set, broader, and big boned. At six-one and a hundred and ninety pounds, I was wide at the shoulders, slimmer elsewhere, but had three inches on him. Our weights were a wash. Overall, an even match.

"Don't think this buys you anything," Tiger said, his eyes angry and resentful.

"Why is it you guys growl in packs, but alone all you do is whine?"

My ally from Kentucky chortled. Tiger scowled and took a swing. I stepped away from it easily. There were snickers from the wrestlers. When I shot a quick look their way, the yaki attacked.

He surged forward with his fists raised and rocketed a punch at my chin. I shuffled away. Grinning, he dogged my steps, jabbing with his left, and bringing his right in low for a rib-crushing uppercut. I sidestepped the jabs, sent his right hand off course with a judo arm sweep and landed a booming left to his jaw.

The yakuza shook his head and backpedaled. His hand slithered toward his ankle. I heard a soft click and polished steel glittered in the yellow light of the locker room.

So much for even odds.

I'd dealt with blades all my life—and hated them. They promised nothing but trouble and were always messy if they connected.

Tiger looped right. I circled left. He swung the knife about vaguely, then rushed forward and lashed out. I backed away. I heard murmurs of protests but my eyes were glued to the metal. I didn't have time to wait for the sympathy vote to roll in.

Tiger waved the weapon in the space between us. "Ain't yappin' now, are you hotshot?"

I let the quip fly by unanswered. Speaking took energy and I needed to concentrate on the gleaming steel. Without warning Tiger darted in again, crossing my field of vision from left to right. I jumped left and as the knife hand slid harmlessly past, I brought my right forearm down on his wrist—and pulled back. He grunted and turned toward me. I answered with a blindside roundhouse already on the way that he met nicely with the middle of his face. I felt the cartilage in his nose collapse. The karate-street combo wasn't my best move but should have put him down.

It didn't.

Twin streams of blood flowed freely from his nose. The yaki must have been hurting, but he didn't let it show. And he'd held onto the knife. Like most of his kind, he was tough and tenacious.

He had a high pain threshold, too.

Without taking his eyes from me, Tiger wiped away the blood with the edge of his palm. Anger swelled his features. He thrust out once or twice with his weapon to keep me at bay while he considered a new plan of attack.

I watched the metal first, his face second.

In his head I saw pride and knew his decision before he made it.

He swung the switchblade halfheartedly, pretending to test the waters, then pounced. As soon as he committed, I shifted into gear. I countered from the other side, batting the inside wrist of his knife hand aside with a left arm sweep before connecting with a solid right to the mid-body. He stumbled back, faltered, then advanced again, a shade slower.

I struck from the left with two quick jabs, then fired a right hook at his chin. I put everything I had behind it. The yaki lieutenant absorbed the blows without noticeable effect at first. His bulbous head with its sculpted good looks bobbed with each strike. He blinked once. His upper body swayed to the rear, tilted forward, then his eyes rolled up into his head and he toppled over sideways.

I waited a beat, and when he didn't stir I nodded my thanks to Kentucky, grabbed the back of Tiger's shirt collar, and dragged him toward the exit. Akeshi still blocked my path. I stared at the chubby-faced young wrestler and he stepped aside.

Out in a new, well-lit hallway I glanced around and said, "There a place I can use?"

From the doorway, Kentucky pointed to the third door on the left. "The general meeting room. Usually empty this time of day."

"That'll do."

I put out my hand and the American-wrestler-turned-sumo smothered my outstretched limb with one of his calloused oversized paws. We exchanged final nods then he turned away. He had a fight to prepare for and so did I.

I dragged my unconscious conquest toward the meeting room.

I left Tiger face down on the floor, still senseless, and called up my second snapshot. With a few swift swipes and pokes I sent the photograph to Noda, asking for an ID on Ascot.

Next, I bent over Tiger and dug through his pockets. I found a pack of Mevius cigarettes, some loose coins, a deerskin wallet, a cell phone, a second knife, and a red plastic lighter with a black silhouette of a shapely lady in partial undress from Club Hot Dream near Tokyo Station. I piled my finds on the conference room table. Tiger groaned and mumbled endearments to a woman called Junko.

I dumped out the contents of the billfold. There was the

equivalent of twelve hundred dollars in Japanese yen and a wad of receipts. One was for a rent-a-car from an agency in the city of Osaka, which didn't surprise me. Yakuza activity flourished in the region. Another was for a hotel room in the same area for three nights. An assortment of chits from pricey drinking spots rounded out the collection. I was looking at the skeletal remains of a business trip for which the yaki lieutenant expected to be reimbursed. Under the bluster and the violence, yakuza gangs were functioning enterprises. Sometimes small, sometimes large, but always in search of cash flow.

I also found a pair of calling cards, one from a realtor and another from someone named Duc Phan, a top-ranked chef at what appeared to be an upscale Vietnamese restaurant. A curious turn. Tiger was a fast-food, ramen type of guy. A note on the card in a feminine hand asked him to call, and left a phone number. Maybe the remnants of a flirtation.

I set the cards aside, hoisted Tiger upright, and slammed him into a chair. Then I slapped each cheek hard. When the yaki opened his eyes, he found the pointed end of his own knife hovering an inch above his right eye.

"Stay very still," I said. "You lose an eye the ladies won't be coming around as much."

He blinked once, and when his mind cleared said, "You know who you're dealing with?"

"Do you?"

"What'chu want?"

"Answers."

"Got only one for you, *gaijin*—no."

The *foreigner* thing again.

"Charming," I said, and made a tight circle with the blade to keep him on point. "Where's the girl?"

Defiant brown eyes stared at me for a moment, then Tiger erupted in laughter, his body jerking sideways to avoid the weapon.

I flicked the steel at his cheek. It wasn't a big cut, but it would bleed. The face always bleeds.

"Let's try this again," I said, moving the knife back to its first target. "Only takes an inch."

His small grubby eyes just glared. He didn't blink, he didn't retreat. What had I missed? I had little to work with. In my pocket my phone buzzed with an incoming call. I moved the point of the blade to the soft, pliant triangle of flesh under Tiger's chin.

"Don't do anything stupid," I said. "If that's possible."

I pulled out my mobile. Noda was on the other end.

"You're slipping, Brodie," he said as soon as I answered.

"Funny. What have you got for me?"

"Guy with Tiger is Minoru Ide. You know him, right?"

"You mean the restaurant mogul?"

"Yeah."

That's why he looked familiar. Ide was a public figure. He appeared at regular intervals in the news and on television talk shows. He owned five or six nationwide chains of family restaurants and an even greater number of *izakaya* pub-style eateries. He represented—no, *was*—Corporate Culinary in Japan.

A promising link to Sato's case—and a potentially toxic one.

"Anything else?" I asked Noda.

"No. Show's all yours," he said and hung up.

Big Culinary...Sushi Sho...Tiger's wallet...

I checked on my hostage, then reached out, curled my arm around his belongings, and dragged them closer. I plucked up one of the business cards and studied it.

New Vietnamese Cuisine
Duc Phan
Executive Chef

6-10-35 Seijo
Setagaya-ku
03-5520-6310
Reservations Suggested

The translation was easy enough: Setagaya was one of Tokyo's most exclusive areas, and Seijo one of its most desirable neighborhoods. And this Duc Phan managed the place. Probably owned it.

In light of Noda's phone call, the card took on an altogether new meaning.

I glanced at Tiger. He avoided my look.

I picked up the *yaki*'s mobile and let the facial recognition sensors scan his features. The software did its job and the locked screen gave way to a cluster of apps. I pulled up the phone function, punched in the handwritten number on Duc Phan's card left by the woman, and listened to the distant ring.

A female voice picked up and said in a soft, breathless voice, "Did you do it? Is he gone? Will he leave us alone?" Fear framed each question like ice crystals around the edge of a window pane. But beneath the fear was anticipation.

A chill crawled up my spine.

"Hello? Takagi-sama?"

Tiger's surname. With an elevated honorific attached. And unequivocal, almost agonizing, deference.

I disconnected.

I'd found the common thread and hated what I'd found. It was nothing like what I'd expected. It was far worse.

I contemplated the voice on the other end of the line. The woman's eagerness and apprehension. Her painfully deprecating politeness. I inhaled noisily, unhappily. Every possible road led to a bad place. I had a clutch of new questions for my captive, but I would need more than physical leverage to squeeze any answers from him.

"Maybe," I said eventually, "I'll hog tie you and dump you on your boss's doorstep. Big demotion he sees his top lieutenant bound and gagged."

A furtive look flittered across Tiger's face. He was making calculations. But not the kind I'd anticipated.

I considered the scorn behind his laughter when I'd asked about Mia. I considered the tenor of his computations. And I considered the stretch limo and the way he'd slid comfortably into the back seat.

Then I put it together: "You're working for yourself this time, aren't you? Behind your boss's back?"

Tiger paled. *Got him.*

Complete allegiance to the gang is a must but Tiger had strayed. He was siphoning off some cream for himself. That kind of betrayal would get him dumped into Tokyo Bay without ceremony. Maybe without hands as well, if his boss chose to make a statement. Yaki bosses were big on flashy punishments that left a lasting impression on the rest of their underlings.

I lowered the knife. "Back off and I go away."

He scoffed. "This play's gonna set me up for life. Nothing you can do about it."

"Sure there is. I'll have a chat with the big man."

His lips twisted into a smirk. "You're a fuckin' *gaijin*. He ain't gonna listen to you."

"Ah, but he will. Particularly when he learns you've been stealing from the group for years. Piled up a lot of money that belongs to him."

His face reddened. "That ain't true."

"But the game you're running on Sushi Sho *is* true. I bring proof of that and your boss will swallow the whole package."

"Not from a *gaijin*."

"So I'll send a Japanese friend. A very convincing one. And for insurance we'll make sure rumors about you hit the grapevine."

His shifty brown eyes careened around the room, looking for an out.

"On the other hand," I said, "if you back off Sato, it all goes away."

"Too much money."

"Can't spend it if you're floating in the bay."

He shrugged. A nerve under his left eye twitched. That's all I needed.

I said, "Game's over, Tiger."

He sneered but the bluster had gone. I'd blocked him at every turn.

"Last question. Where's the girl?"

"In hiding with her boyfriend."

"Lucky for you if she is."

"She is."

"So she's safe."

"For now."

I scowled at his threat and pushed the blade into the fold of his lower eyelid until I could feel his eyeball offering its firm, liquid resistance. Another millimeter and I'd puncture the cornea.

Tiger scrambled upward in his seat to get away from the steel but my hand rose with him. His eyes bulged.

I said, "I've got twenty people behind me and friends working for the Tokyo PD. By tomorrow all of them will know your story.

You come after me, you're dead."

He was straining so hard to catch a glimpse of the knife, I couldn't be sure he'd heard me.

I shoved the blade under his nose. "Did you hear what I said?"

He nodded, a scarlet teardrop of blood forming beneath his right eye.

"I need an answer I can hear, Tiger."

"Yeah, I heard ya."

"Good, 'cause next time the knife doesn't stop."

I flung the weapon across the room and walked out.

A solitary mustard yellow light glowed behind the snow-white paper of the shoji screens at Sushi Sho. It was late. All the customers had wandered home, replete after their three-star meal. I too wanted to get home, which tonight meant back to my daughter.

But I wasn't quite done yet.

As I approached Sato's place I heard simmering murmurs inside. I cracked open the sliding door maybe an eighth of an inch. In the distant, post-dining gloom I saw father, mother, and daughter gathered at a table against the far wall.

"He's from a good family, Mama," Mia said. She was back.

Mrs. Sato shook her head.

"But, Mama..." Mia was crying.

Sato's wife pursed her lips. "He's not one of us."

As they talked, a kaleidoscope of emotions played across their faces. Mia's features faded from an amber honey to a milky white. "The world is changing every day, Mama. Please."

"Not in this house. Not today, not ever. We're ninth generation."

The kindly matriarchal visage that had looked on with such pleasure as Jenny unwrapped the varicolored top now churned with fury, and allowed no room for compromise.

Ninth generation, and you nearly destroyed it all, it said.

Mia turned desperate eyes toward her father. "Papa?"

Sato darted a panicked look between the two women in his life. His wife held the upper hand. Her parents hadn't produced a male heir, so Sato married into the family to carry on the lineage and lucrative sushi shop. He'd been the stopgap to a traditional Japanese problem.

"Papa?" Mia asked again. "Please do something."

A cold gust rattled the shop widows as I watched a family rip itself apart. The wife and daughter hadn't noticed my arrival. But Sato, the ever-attentive chef, had. In desperation he turned his doughy face in my direction. "Good timing, Brodie. Come in and join us. Our daughter has returned."

I pushed the door aside and entered. "How about that."

The chef blushed at the slight, but his composure didn't slip. There was too much at stake. "You heard what we were talking about. Can you help me out?"

Mrs. Sato shot me a warning look. Mia gazed my way, her eyes bloodshot and hopeful.

I inhaled deeply. Sato's request was way above my pay grade. He was asking me to reopen an old wound—the wound I would always carry. I wanted to refuse, but another glance at Mia and my resistance melted.

I sighed. "Twelve years ago I married Mieko. You all knew her. Even though—" I paused, searching for the right phrasing, "—she didn't look like me, didn't talk like me, didn't come from the same country as me, we fell in love. It wasn't planned. I'd never dated anyone outside 'my own kind,' so to speak, but it just happened. We had Jenny two years later. Two years after that I was a widower. Today, I look back at that time as a gift I wouldn't trade for anything. I feel the same way about Jenny. I have no misgivings, no regrets, and I never will."

Mrs. Sato shot up from her chair, her hands pushing at the air as if she could shove my words aside. "This is not the same. Not the same at all."

Plump tears streamed down Mia's face. "It's exactly the same, Mama, only he's Vietnamese, not Japanese. He's a kind man, and a wonderful chef. Like papa."

Mrs. Sato's eyes were damp. Tears shimmered at their corners but didn't fall. "I won't allow it. I just can't."

"Mama, please. Won't you—"

"No!"

Mia froze, her lips parted in mid-sentence. The force of her mother's retort had stunned her. Mrs. Sato glared openly now. Proud and unapologetic. Conceding nothing.

"Mama…"

"No."

A softer tone the second time, but equally unyielding. The boundaries of her soul had been set long ago. Held captive by the needs of the family legacy.

Mia's head sank. She slid her palms absently over her thighs, smoothing imaginary wrinkles from her skirt. Her breath steadied. Her weeping ceased. In increments, she regained her composure. No one spoke. Mia took a deep breath, biding her time, giving her mother a last chance to relent. Or her father a chance to find his courage.

But her mother wouldn't, and her father couldn't.

Mia rose to her feet. Sato watched helplessly. Mrs. Sato wrenched her gaze away. Mia wiped the wet, glistening tracks from her cheeks. She raised her head and walked purposely to the exit, each step a declaration. She pushed aside the sliding partition. She looked back at her parents. She waited. Said nothing. Her face was a pale oval against the blackness of the night.

Neither parent spoke. Neither moved.

Mia nodded once to herself. A fire kindled in her eyes. Her resolve jelled. She would move forward. Would eventually go to the man she'd chosen. They'd start a new life, and the tenth generation would find a new way.

The next instant she stepped into the night and was gone.

All these years people thought that Sushi Sho had three stars. But there had only ever been one. And it wasn't the chef.

Sato shot an accusing look at his wife. "You said I needed to hand over twenty percent of the shop to your sister for family reasons, but it was that yakuza guy."

"You knew the truth."

"I only guessed it after a while. You lied to me."

"I was trying to save our daughter."

"At the expense of all I've worked for? There are other ways."

"Twenty percent is nothing to save the family's honor. And it was the only way to scare away that *Vietnamese* man."

"What if they had done what you asked…permanently?"

Mrs. Sato lowered her eyes but not before I caught a flash of guilt under her icy glare. "How they do their business is none of mine."

"What are you talking about? They tricked you. Can't you see that?"

"I don't care."

Sato had discovered the truth somewhere along the line, but found himself trapped between the clashing ideals of two stronger women. His solution? Get me to pull the yakuza off their backs. I'd untangled the immediate problem but clearly not the long-running one: the dry rot festering in the House of Sato.

"So the boy's a little different," the brow-beaten chef said. "What's the harm if our daughter's happy?"

"It's not *your* heritage. It's a disgrace I could never allow. Everyone would know."

I listened without comment, and they let me. I'd already witnessed the worst of it.

"You're crazy. They would have taken everything in the end. The shop and our land. And now we've lost Mia."

All of which was true.

But Sato had stopped short of admitting his own role in Mia's departure. He had been a rising young sushi chef when he took the reins of Sushi Sho. Over the ensuing three decades he'd sharpened his art and raised the shop's profile. He knew the precise temperature at which to serve tuna *while* accounting for the soft radiating warmth of rice underneath. He knew the ideal thickness for teasing out the succulence of scallops. He had disassembled and reassembled every type of sushi a thousand times to find the sweet spot of each. His talent and perseverance had earned him three stars. He'd drawn on a certain kind of fortitude to reach such heights but it came at the expense of his home life. After giving up his own name to assume the mantle of the Sato family, he'd never recovered his sense of self. Never righted his personal compass. Or maybe it had never been right to start with.

A family rotting from within is easy prey for a renegade yaki like Tiger. And he leapt at the chance.

This play's gonna set me up for life.

Sato's shop and neighboring home rested on prime Tokyo real estate. On the open market the joint properties would fetch a mid-seven-figure price tag, in U.S. dollars, maybe more. Throw in Sushi Sho's blue-chip reputation and the combination would be iresistible, so Tiger brought in a real estate agent to assess their value. The realtor's business card in his wallet told me that, and more. Tiger next used the agent's estimate to negotiate a fee that would set him up for life if he delivered twenty percent of Sushi Sho to the restaurant magnate. A fee Tiger had clung to until I'd pried it loose.

But those weren't the final pieces of the puzzle.

It's my daughter, Mia, Sato had said at the start. *I need you to find her.* I'd taken the master chef at his word, but when I'd pressured Tiger his laugh had gone ballistic.

Mia Sato had never been in physical danger. Only her boyfriend had. She had never been abducted. Sato led me in that direction to draw me in. Mia's only crime had been to fall in love with someone outside her tribe. And she'd gone to him when he went into hiding to escape Tiger's threats.

The idea of a Vietnamese son-in-law clearly horrified Mrs. Sato. She had no doubt tried to dissuade her daughter but when motherly persuasion failed, Mrs. Sato had grown desperate. And desperation led her to into Tiger's hands.

Yakuza gangs often act as fixers. Intimidation, extortion, strikebreaking, you name it. Whatever pressure point needs to be pushed, for the right price they'll push it. Mrs. Sato would have found Tiger through some common channel. The yaki saw an opportunity to parlay her maternal turmoil into a windfall, and almost succeeded.

I figured he roughed up the boyfriend but pulled his punches, then told Mrs. Sato that Duc Phan wouldn't give up Mia so easily. When Mrs. Sato offered more money, Tiger said the boy might have to be killed and upped his price to twenty percent of the shop.

Mrs. Sato took the bait. I'd like to think she resisted or had second thoughts somewhere along the line. That a cautionary note sounded in her soul. Maybe she reconsidered and tried to back away but Tiger pressured her, or fanned her fears. But whatever the twists and turns of the negotiation, in the end Mrs. Sato accepted the yaki's deal.

For me, the solution arrived in two stages: first, Noda's revelation about the restaurant mogul; then, in that light, the importance of Duc Phan's card in Tiger's wallet. Once I made the link, I recalled where I'd seen the handwriting on the card—and punched in the number. It hadn't belonged to one of Tiger's female admirers.

Mrs. Sato had answered the call I'd made from the yaki lieutenant's phone.

And she had asked if it was done. If Duc Phan was dead.

There'd been no regret in her voice.

I hadn't seen any as she'd rebuffed her daughter's tear-laden pleas.

There was no room in Mrs. Sato's rainbow for a new color. She wanted everything in her world spinning smoothly, as it had for nine long generations. That had been the silent message her husband had sent when he invited me for sushi. It wasn't that Mia was missing. It was that his wife had trapped him in an ever-tightening web spun without mercy.

BOOKS BY NICK KOLAKOWSKI

NOW AVAILABLE!
THE LOVE & BULLETS HOOKUP SERIES

COMING
SUMMER 2018

Another winner or finalist of most of the major awards that are out there, Art is a steady presence at most of the larger conferences every year. As prolific as he is talented, I've never read an Art Taylor story that didn't impress me. His work is also a regular in anthologies, other magazines, and I can't tell you how happy I am to be able to present the first of hopefully many stories by Art here in D&O:TM. His "novel in stories," On the Road with Del and Louise, was published in 2015 by Henery Press. Otherwise, you can find more of his stories in many of the "Best of" anthologies that have been released the past few years. When I first read this story it reminded me of a famous one by the legendary Richard Matheson. Something about the feel of it. That sure works for me...

Sunday Morning, Saturday Night
Art Taylor

You know one of my favorite things from when I was a kid? Sunday mornings.

Half-awake and all bleary-eyed, grabbing that raggedy blue bear I used to have, the one I'd gnawed the fur off of, toddling down the hall to my parents' room—my mom and my stepdad, that is, never sure where my real dad had gone to. Climbing in bed between them, snuggling against my mom, nestling into her shoulder, feeling the closeness, the warmth. Light sneaking around the blinds, cutting through the shadows and the darkness, and that down comforter of theirs thick against the cold, the way my stepdad kept the heat turned down, and then these whispers from my mom, always telling me how I was her special little man.

Those Sundays—they were the best times of my life.

And then there was the time that my mom and my stepdad were doing *something else* when I toddled in. I mean: bleary-eyed to wide-eyed in a second, even less!

But that's another story, don't you think?

***

Sunday mornings these days, all grown-up, those feelings are harder to come by. Most Sundays it's just me and an empty apartment and the light too bright against some hangover and my eyes shut tight against some dark stirrings in my gut.

Most Sundays.

But some Sundays feel different—this one right now, I mean, and as soon as my eyes open, I see why: a pair of shoes, the shadows of them in the dim light, tossed to the floor but one still upright, standing tall.

"Heeled Oxfords"—that's what the girl had told me last night at the bar. Wingtips. Two-toned, white and black.

Heeled saddle shoes, really, that's what I thought. But I didn't correct her.

"I like your shoes," I'd told her when I first came up—as good a pick-up line as any. Women love their shoes, right? And then, "What do you call them?" and that's when she told me.

"Nice," I told her, and I meant it. She laughed as I said it, shook her head.

"What?" Being laughed at, that sometimes strikes me wrong—happens to all of us, am I right?

"These shoes." She lifted her foot. Her calves tightened. "Always get the guys' attention. Something a little formal about them, proper even, but off-beat too, which men like. Innocence and experience. Subdued but sexy. Madonna and whore. Why do all you men find that such an irresistible combination?"

I'll admit it: I'm slow at working through my own thoughts, reflecting on why I feel the way I do, but everything she was saying, it made sense all of a sudden. She had bright red hair, and this spray of freckles across her cheeks and nose, something innocent about that too. Fresh-faced. Girl next door. You know what I mean. Maybe, seeing that thought through, eventually, good girl gone bad. And peeking out from the cut of her blouse were these exquisite collarbones.

I wanted to take her home, and I told her that—"I want to take you home"—and long story short, even though it looked like she might've been interested in this other guy she was talking to, I eventually got her to accept my invitation, back to that lonely little apartment of mine, a little less lonely for a while.

Longer story short, those heeled, two-toned Oxfords gave a good grip, that innocence and experience again in the mix, being how she had them on through the end, me spreading them one as far from the other as I could before pulling them off for good, before I set out to discover what she was really made of.

I tried to get her to whisper that she loved me, but that might've been overly ambitious on my part.

The sunrise is slicing through the blinds now, cutting through the darkness. I feel its warmth against my back, or maybe it's the warmth of her body, and I press back against her, try to catch some of the intimacy I've been missing, that warmth that I know won't stay. But I keep my eyes on those shoes instead of turning to look at her head-on, the cut of those collarbones, those freckles, that red hair, that bright spray of red.

That other Sunday morning I was talking about, walking in on my mom and my stepdad, walking in on something I didn't understand...I'd said that was another story, but I guess it's really not.

What I saw that morning, what I felt—it was a mystery. My stepdad was growling, "I'm close, I'm close"—but really my mom was far away, rising high above him, her back arched away too. The room was blazing hot, or maybe I just felt hot, but the pale of mom's back looked ice cold—and maybe that was why she yanked the down comforter up so quick. And then—this struck me so strange—right before she pulled those covers up, like a curtain, like a shield, I caught a glimpse of the lace-up boots she was wearing, the ones my stepdad liked to talk about after his third or fourth beer.

Boots in bed? Why in the world?

I almost could've laughed—except that funny feeling I was feeling? It wasn't really funny.

This switch from her whispering that she loved me to shouting down for me to "Get back!" and "Go away!" and "Stop! Stop!" Was it betrayal—what she was doing? Was it that I felt like any love she gave to *him* was less she gave to *me*? Where did the line get crossed from shock to hurt? From hurt to anger? From anger to—

Well, like I said, I'm not real quick at analyzing myself, but I could feel it even then as I swung that little blue bear over and over against her back—could feel with each hit how much I wished already that it was made of stronger, sharper stuff.

THE STANDALONE NOVELS OF ANTHONY NEIL SMITH

ALSO BY THE AUTHOR

THE ADEM & MUSFATA SERIES
ALL THE YOUNG WARRIORS
ONCE A WARRIOR

THE BILLY LAFITTE SERIES
YELLOW MEDICINE
HOGDOGGIN'
THE BADDEST ASS
HOLY DEATH

A Few Cents A Word
Rick Ollerman

This time around I'm going to tell you a story. I'm calling it a story because some of the pieces have been made up, not by me, but mainly by the principals themselves, who are long since dead and gone. Researchers and scholars have attempted to come up with a definitive account of the life of Raoul Falconia Whitfield (1896-1945) but their efforts have fallen largely incomplete. It was almost as though Whitfield was trying to obfuscate his past purposely, nudging future biographers into discouragement. He provided different years for the date of his birth, for instance, and he started presenting his middle name as the romanticize "Fauconier," while his first wife mysteriously went from being named Prudence Smith before they were married to suddenly becoming Prudence Van Tine. Much fancier, to be sure, and indeed, perhaps that may have been the point.

Whitfield the man lived and portrayed an exaggerated version of himself. Did he fly in World War I as he claimed? Certainly, but he did so towing targets and ferrying cargo, not as a fighting lieutenant on combat missions. He cut quite a figure afterwards in Gertrude Stein's salon in Paris. He met other writers there, like Ernest Hemingway, F. Scott Fitzgerald, and Dashiell Hammett. Whitfield and Hammett not only became friends and drinking buddies, later they'd go off through the streets of New York, getting hammered and talking about writing through to the early hours. One fact was that Whitfield, who was at that time one of the most popular and best paid writers in the world wrote letters to his editors at Black Mask recommending strongly that they publish more of his friend, Hammett.

Carroll John Daly, Whitfield, Hammett, and Frederick Nebel are arguably the four voices most responsible for the development of the hard-boiled voice in crime fiction. Something happened to Whitfield, though, that effectively stalled, then killed his career: he came into even more money. More money than he could ever have dreamed of making as a writer of crime fiction.

Whitfield divorced his first wife, Prudence (who later became Hammett's long-time lover—or maybe not so much later), and became the third husband of prominent socialite Emily Davies Vander-bilt Thayer. She brought the money and when it came out went Whitfield's writing ambition. The two started a ranch in Las Vegas, New Mexico, they called "Dead Horse." One of the ways Raoul spent his wife's money was to install an actual polo field. Nice and level and green—in the middle of the desert.

The couple were married just shy of two years. Emily and Raoul had become estranged and while Raoul was supposedly away in Los Angeles, Emily died, inside the locked house at Dead Horse. A gun was found near her right side.

The bullet had entered her left side.

The trajectory of the bullet was pointing at an odd angle for a person who may have shot herself. It had penetrated upward, through her lung and into her heart.

But with the doors being locked from the inside, the separated husband being in another state, and no other suspects, motives, or opportunities presenting themselves, the hastily convened coroner's jury returned a verdict of suicide.

It didn't stop people from talking, or the newspapers from talking cover up.

Emily's death stopped the divorce decree from being finalized, the one that would have cut off the flow of money from Raoul.

When he was writing, Whitfield wrote a number of series and used several names, including "Temple Field" and "Ramon Decolta," the name he used for his PI stories featuring Filipino private investigator Jo Gar. Whitfield's career as a novelist was more uneven than his successful and influential one as a short story writer. For the longer works he took several of his short stories and strung them together, then added material to turn them into "novels." They are often difficult to follow and don't quite hang together in that form, but still, his hard-boiled prose and terse, punchy sentences are still there.

Although Emily Whitfield had filed for divorce the February prior to her death, it hadn't been finalized at the time of her passing so it worked out so that everything fell to Raoul. As an inveterate ladies' man, he had already taken up with a local waitress, Lois Bell. They quickly wed and Raoul resettled them both in California.

Raoul and Lois couldn't outlive the rumors from his previous union but that didn't stop the pair of them from traveling the world and living the high life. Running out of Emily's money did. Dead Horse had been sold off and Raoul had contracted tuberculosis and was living in a sanatorium. At the time, remember, there were no antibiotics and Hammett, a consumption survivor himself, who was still somewhat in correspondence with Raoul, wrote about the inner strength needed to overcome the disease. He told his lover, Prue Whitfield (Raoul's first wife), that he wasn't sure if Raoul had it. Twice Hammett told Lillian Hellman, his acknowledged companion throughout most of his life, that he'd sent Whitfield checks of $500 to see him through; he asked her not to be mad. It seems as though Hellman wasn't fond of Whitfield. At one point it actually seemed that Whitfield believed he had a chance of being released from the hospital.

In September of 1943 Lois Bell Whitfield, nearly twenty years Raoul's junior, "jumped" from her hotel window while her husband was in the hospital. In his letters to Lillian Hellman about it, Hammett was always guarded about how the words he used when discussing it. Hammett learned about it from Prue Whitfield and it was she who used the quotes around "jumped" in her letters. About two weeks later, Lois Bell died. After the death of Emily at Dead Horse there were even more questions about Raoul, but it was hard to dispute his presence in the hospital.

That's two wives for Raoul Whitfield, one "suicide," and one apparent suicide. In his novel, Dead Horse, *the wonderful writer Walter Satterthwait took it upon himself to research as much as he could the actual facts of Raoul, Emily, Lois and Dead Horse Ranch. The answers couldn't be contained in a non-fiction book, and indeed Satterthwait did us all one better. In his novel, he provided a surmise that not only fits the facts as well as anyone could know them, he offers a diabolical and clever solution to the mystery of who exactly killed Emily, and how.*

Just remember that while Raoul had not been an actual fighter pilot in WWI, he had been a pilot.

Remember that while he was out of town the night Emily died, he was reasonably close by, in Los Angeles.

Since the divorce had not yet been finalized, Whitfield had his own set of keys to the ranch house.

And remember that polo field? The one Raoul had installed at the ranch, that oasis of green in the middle of the desert? Satterthwait said it was so big, you could land a plane right on it.

Check out his book, Dead Horse. *He's a heckuva writer.*

And so is Raoul Whitfield, one of the original hard-boiled innovators. He wasn't one to shy away from fast and sudden violence. If he had somehow been involved with Emily's death, perhaps that fact contributed to his suffering, alone in a TB hospital, living much of the time inside his own head, for nearly the last two years of his life.

Much of the action in Whitfield's Jo Gar series takes place off screen and gives the effect of Whitfield almost having cut pieces of the story out deliberately so that he can spring the entire solution of the crime on the reader at the end. The story included here, "Death on the Pasig," is the second Jo Gar story, first published in Black Mask *in the March 30, 1930 issue. I chose this one in particular because this technique of Whitfield's is less in evidence here than in other stories, and the effect can sometimes be jarring.*

Death on the Pasig
A Jo Gar Story
Raoul Whitfield

The Island detective takes up a trail of justice and vengeance...

The ceiling fans stirred hot air and made faint creaking sounds as they turned slowly. Shrill, native voices reached the café from the blue-gray eyes on the tall glass of lemonade he was sipping at intervals. It was about as hot as he had ever remembered! Baguio would be better because of the altitude. Or perhaps an inter-Island trip would help.

He raised his eyes to the bulk of Ben Rannis, noted that the manager of the Manila Hotel was pale, very pale. As Rannis stood near the screened doors and searched the café with his dark eyes, Jo Gar raised his right hand slowly and moved it from side to side. It was a languid motion—that of one who has spent many years in the tropics and has learned to conserve energy.

Rannis saw him, moved swiftly towards the table. He weighed more than two hundred; he was a powerful man. There wasn't much stomach, but he had broad shoulders and a great chest. He was several inches over six feet. Perspiration streaked his heavy face; he pulled a chair from the table, set it down closer to the one Jo Gar occupied.

"You appear ill—and you hurry too much. What is it?"

The Island detective spoke almost tonelessly. His English was precise. He was small in size, and his gray hair contrasted his brown, young face strangely. His slightly almond-shaped eyes were only half opened.

Rannis muttered something that sounded like a curse. He was

breathing hard; it was almost as though he had been running along the Escolta.

"The Cleyo Maru's in," he said in his husky voice. "Got in two hours ago. Craise was aboard. He sent me a message. It was given to me over the phone by a Filipino who acted damned cheerful about it. He said 'Meester Craise has arrived. He wishes me to tell you that information has come to him. You are in great danger. It is better to leave the city at once.' Then he hung up."

Jo Gar frowned. "It was Craise's brother you killed, two months ago, I think," he said steadily.

Rannis groaned. "You know damned well it was, Jo," he replied. "And you know damned well Howard Craise is out to get me for it. One way or another. And it was an accident."

The Island detective shrugged his shoulders slightly. He smiled with his thin lips.

"You had been drinking," he reminded. "John Craise was not strong. You struck him very hard."

"He'd been drinking, too. He called me a nasty name. That all came out at the trial. Howard Craise knows all that, even if he was in England at the time."

Jo Gar sipped more of his lemonade. He turned his browned face slightly away from the hotel manager.

"That is so," he agreed. "And now he is not in England. He is in Manila. You have been called and told your life is endangered. Recently you have killed John Craise and have been acquitted of the charge of murder."

The hotel manager turned narrowed eyes towards Gar's. He said hoarsely: "He'll kill me, Jo. I can't shoot. I want you to go to him, tell him how it was. You'd just come in on that transport—you worked the case. He knows you—he'll believe you."

The Island detective smiled with faint mockery in his eyes.

"You did not intend to murder his brother," he said slowly, tonelessly. "I feel certain of that."

Ben Rannis shoved back his chair and rose. His voice was shaken, uncertain. But he kept it fairly low.

"He's at his brother's place—fix it up, Jo. He'll get brooding—in this damned heat—"

His voice broke. Fear was gripping the big man, and Jo Gar hated to see fear in a man's eyes. He said slowly: "I will go to him.

Where will you go?"

Rannis swore. "Along the river—got to get a drink. Keep away from the hotel until you see him. The heat'll get him thinking—"

He turned, went slowly from the soft drink café. His fingers were twitching at his sides. Jo Gar shook his head very slowly. He finished his iced lemonade. His slitted eyes watched Rannis go through the screened doors, merge with the crowd on the Escolta; Filipinos, Chinese, Japanese, English, Spaniards—and a scattering of Americans, mostly Army men.

Jo Gar sighed. He was aware of the fact, now made definite, that Benjamin Rannis was a coward. He was afraid of death, and yet he had killed. And the Island detective had given him a promise.

There was difficulty in getting the connection, nothing was done hurriedly in the Islands. A Chinese servant answered the phone. He was not sure that his master would speak with Señor Gar. His master was sleeping. Yes, he knew it was past siesta hours, but his master was very weary. He would see about the matter.

Jo Gar held the receiver, waited. Several minutes passed. Then a voice came to him. It possessed a slightly English accent. It was a heavy-toned voice.

"Are you there? Howard Craise speaking."

The Island detective said slowly: "It is Señor Gar. You perhaps remember me in matters of the Island police. I would like to come to you, talk with you. It is the matter of your brother's death."

He paused. There was silence at the other end. Then the voice sounded again. It seemed colder in tone.

"At six, say? Here, at the house?"

Jo Gar watched a carromatta pass, in the street. The pony was white. He said:

"At six, thank you. I will arrive."

He heard the click of the receiver at the other end. The Craise house was beyond the Walled City, perhaps a mile along the Bay. It was a fine old place. Spanish, built many years ago. The Craise brothers owned plantations, not on Luzon but further south.

The Island detective left the café. It was almost five, but the heat was still very severe. He turned off the Escolta, moved down a narrow, winding street towards the Pasig. Behind him there was the clatter of a pony's hoofs. A native voice shrilled at the animal, urging greater speed. Jo Gar stepped into an evil-smelling doorway, turned. The carromatta passed close to the broken curbing; he saw the driver clearly. Back of the little seat, in the interior of the small, two-wheeled carriage, he saw another figure. Then the carromatta was beyond him, going rapidly towards the river Pasig.

Jo Gar stepped from the doorway, looked for another conveyance. There was none in sight. He sighed heavily. One could not answer a telephone three miles from the Escolta—and yet arrive on a narrow street just off the Escolta two minutes later. For that reason Jo Gar was very anxious to keep track of the carromatta which had just passed him, bearing as a passenger Howard Craise.

In five minutes he obtained a carromatta, gave the driver instructions. There was no sign of the two-wheeled conveyance in which he had seen Howard Craise. After a half hour tour of the narrow streets running towards the Pasig from the Escolta, Jo Gar descended and paid the driver. It was slightly cooler; he would sip another iced drink, hire another carromatta and go out to the Craise house. Filipinos could gossip; he did not wish to give his last driver the opportunity to talk—not with some servant in the vicinity of the Craise home.

He had his drink, hailed a native driving a good sized pony, and was driven at fair speed to the Craise house on the Bay. The Island of Cavite could be plainly seen; Jo stood on the wide porch and frowned at it. When the Chinese servant opened the door, however, he was smiling.

He waited less than five minutes in a large room that was almost cool. Howard Craise came downstairs rather noisily; he was medium in size with blond hair and blue eyes. He was dressed in a suit of white duck, but he did not look so cool.

"I awakened you?" The Island detective smiled at him.

Craise shook his head. He seemed a little nervous. He had a peculiar way of blinking his eyes, as though he were in bright sunlight rather than in a dark room.

"I was reading—lying around and reading," he said. "Good to be ashore, we had a rough passage."

Jo Gar nodded. "I will arrive directly at the object of my call," he said. "Mister Benjamin Rannis has been murdered."

He watched Craise's body jerk—watched the right hand come upward, then relax. He saw the blue eyes widen, narrow again. And then Howard Craise spoke: "But it's only been—"

He checked himself. The Island detective nodded, smiling pleasantly.

"A very short time since you had your Filipino boy call and threaten him," he finished. "That is true."

Craise was staring at him. His fists clenched; there was sudden anger in his eyes. He spoke in a hard tone: "You're accusing me of killing Rannis? You mean to tell me—"

Jo Gar looked hurt. He moved his head from side to side, slowly.

"He was murdered while you were sleeping, or reading," he pointed out. "But it was unwise of you to have your servant threaten him. He has probably told several people of the matter."

Howard Craise wet his lips with the tip of his tongue. He smiled nastily.

"Of course no servant of mine called him and threatened him. That's absurd. If it's circumstantial evidence you are counting on—"

He checked himself again. Rage was in his eyes. Jo Gar bowed slightly.

"I admire the way you think, Señor," he said quietly. "Circumstantial evidence is quite unsatisfactory—in the Islands, of course. I merely wanted to inform you—"

The bell tinkled. Silently the Chinese servant went to the door. He opened it, stepped aside. Juan Arragon, of the City police, his fat face a brown mask, came toward them. He nodded towards Jo Gar, bowed to Howard Craise.

"Will you be so kind as to come with me to the City?" he asked.

"We have just taken the body of Mister Benjamin Rannis from the Pasig River. He is dead, perhaps murdered. You are, implicated. My superiors are anxious that you—"

Craise smiled with his lips. "Frame-up, eh?" he muttered. "Of course I'll come—Wong, my helmet!"

He moved towards the square reception hall. Juan Arragon let his eyes meet Jo Gar's.

"You do not seem surprised—to learn of Mister Rannis' death," he said slowly.

Jo Gar smiled. "I had just informed Señor Craise accordingly," he said simply.

He watched Arragon's eyes narrow in surprise. The Manila police officer was no fool. He said very quietly: "I came here very rapidly. In a machine. The body was just discovered. Yet you already knew?"

Jo Gar said slowly: "Why did you come here so quickly?"

The fat-faced officer smiled a little. His voice was very smooth as he replied:

"There was certain evidence."

The Island detective nodded. "That was my reason for coming here without knowing that Señor Rannis had been murdered," he said very slowly. "There was certain evidence."

Jo Gar sat in the fan-backed, wicker chair, made by prisoners in Bilibid, and smiled faintly into the eyes of Juan Arragon. It was much cooler—tropical night had dropped over Manila. He spoke in a soft, steady tone.

"Señor Rannis was a coward, plainly. He did, however, give me work at times. I had promised to help him. He came to me in the café, afraid of Howard Craise. He had reason to fear the brother of the man he had struck down so hard that his fist caused death. I agreed to intercede. I called the Craise house, and I was answered by a servant who informed me he did not like to disturb his master. That was an untruth, you say. You tell me that Howard Craise did not speak to me at the time I mention—that you saw him in a carromatta only a few minutes later, driving towards the Pasig."

The Manila police officer nodded, showed white teeth in a smile.

"Perhaps you saw him, also," he said softly. "You went to his home, informed him that Señor Rannis had been murdered, before you knew that. There was a reason. You are clever, yes?"

Jo Gar chuckled. "We are both clever," he qualified. "And so is Howard Craise."

Juan Arragon shrugged his shoulders. "I do not see in what manner," he said. "He has a servant threaten a man he is bound to hate. He has another talk over the telephone for him. And he allows both you and me to see him riding towards the spot where the body of the man he threatened is dragged from the Pasig. Is that clever?"

The Island detective gestured with his hands spreading out, palms up.

"He allows us both to see him, you say," he observed slowly. "Perhaps it is very, very clever!"

He rose slowly, reached for his pith helmet. Arragon was watching him curiously. They were friends of old. Five years ago, before he had become a private investigator, Jo Gar had worked on the Manila police force.

"We are handling Mister Craise with what the Americans call the gloves," Arragon said slowly. "He is friendly with many important personages. He dines at Señor Carlysle's home. We must be careful, but sincere."

Jo Gar nodded. Arnold Carlysle was the American who headed the police force, an organization combining Americans and Filipinos. There were times when the solution of crime, in Manila, was a delicate affair.

"There were two knife wounds," Arragon went on. "One in the back, almost between the shoulder blades. The other just over the heart. Chinos on the junk near the shore heard the splash. One of them went overboard for the body. Mister Rannis had taken drinks at Manuelo's—two or three. He had left, saying he was much in need of air. There are many river boats, junks and sampans, anchored side by side within a square of Manuelo's. I feel that Mister Craise could have reached the junk near which the splash was heard within three minutes after the time I saw him riding in the carromatta. I feel that murder was committed shortly after these three minutes. Señor Craise possessed a motive."

Jo Gar smiled faintly. It amused him to note the application of "Señor" and "mister" to an Englishman. Arragon had Spanish blood in his veins, as did the Island detective. Forms of address were confusing.

He stood near the door of Arragon's office, facing the police officer. He said slowly: "Señor Craise had much time, before he arrived in Manila, to cool his anger. He is a shrewd man. Circumstantial evidence is all against him. I will be honest with you. I, too, saw him riding towards the Pasig. Ben Rannis came to me in fear of him. He had a reason for his fear. I was answered from the house—but Señor Craise could not have been two places at once. Much of our evidence rests on what we saw with our own eyes. Perhaps others saw him, too. Supposing then, with one twist he could destroy this evidence—"

He paused. Arragon nodded his head and made clicking sounds with his tongue.

"It is difficult," he agreed. "I, too, believe he might have desired us to see him. And others to see him. He has been questioned, released. He has returned to his home. Silbino is strolling near the house. What next?"

Jo Gar placed his pith helmet over his gray hair. He smiled almost cheerfully.

"A poet once wrote: 'There is mystery in the black-watered Pasig,'" he said. "I shall go towards the river, because the poet is accurate. It is so."

Juan Arragon fanned himself slowly with a stained palm leaf, and rolled his little eyes towards the ceiling of the office.

"It is damn so!" he said softly.

Manuelo's was a shack not far from the river—perhaps a hundred feet up a narrow alley. It was frequented by coolies, half-breed Spaniards, low class Filipinos, and others of the river. Manuelo himself was a small, emaciated human. He had bad teeth and a scarred face. His fingers were long and bony.

He repeated a good many times that the Americano Rannis had come in for a drink. It had been sake, he thought. He could not remember. Many rivermen had crowded his place. He said that Rannis had looked very sick. He had not stayed long. Manuelo was not sure of the time. Señor Rannis had needed air. He had gone away. No, Manuelo did not know Señor Craise. He had never come to the place.

And that was about all. The Chinos on the junk had difficulty in talking with Gar. They were not sure where the body had struck the water. They pointed at the spot where Rannis' body had been seen—the one who had gone overboard said that he thought Rannis had moved his arms a little. But not after he had reached the Americano.

After two hours along the Pasig, Jo Gar sighed and muttered to himself.

"It is always so with the river Pasig. So little seen or heard. And it was not dark, even. Supposing, now, another than Howard Craise had been in that carromatta?"

It was a thought, but he did not care much about it. There would have to be a remarkable similarity of humans. He had been fooled. Juan Arragon had been fooled. No, he did not think that. They were both familiar with Craise.

He called Arragon's office from a little tobacco shop just off the Escolta. Juan's voice held an excited note.

"Come to me at once!" he urged. "Here in my office we have the murderer of Señor Rannis! He has confessed."

Ten minutes later Jo Gar entered the office. His eyes went from the khaki colored uniforms of the two Filipino police to the figure slumped over the desk. Juan Arragon said sharply: "Donnell—up!"

The man raised his head, turned slightly, stared at the Island detective. Jo Gar sucked in his breath, muttered to himself.

"Marie! But they—are alike!"

This man's hair was a dirtier blond color. His eyes were bloodshot, larger than Señor Craise's. He was more stooped—and looked older. But there was similarity—great similarity. In the carromatta, seated erect, they could have been easily mistaken.

"He is—one Donnell. A sort of beachcomber," Arrogan said slowly, a trace of excitement in his voice. "My men found him cowering across the Pasig from the scene of the crime. We have the knife—he tossed it away as they closed in. He has confessed. It was a terrible scheme—he knew of his resemblance to Howard Craise. For months he has awaited the Señor's return. He has threatened Señor Rannis, again and again. He got into the carromatta after siesta time today, drove towards Manuelo's. He knew that Señor Rannis went there. When Rannis came from the place he followed him to the river, knifed him, dragged him across the junks—threw him overboard. He made his escape. Later, when we were bringing Señor Craise to trial, he planned to give himself up, tell what he had done for sufficient money. Many thousands of dollars. He would force Señor Craise to pay—and then he intended to get away with the money. And not to confess. A tremendous scheme!"

The man who resembled Howard Craise dropped his head in his arms. He cried out hoarsely: "Let me go—into the Bay! The sharks—"

He had a broken, husky voice. His body looked thinner than Craise's. Collapsed across Juan Arragon's desk he was a pitiful figure of a beaten man.

"Do they not look alike?" Arrogan asked grimly.

"You see, after the murder his nerve deserted him. He went to pieces. Is it not fortunate we were careful with Señor Craise? You see he did speak with you over the telephone.

Jo Gar nodded his head slowly. The phone bell rang. Arragon answered it. He smiled. His white teeth showed.

"I will come soon to your home, Señor Craise," he said into the mouthpiece. "I have news of importance. I will be there within the half hour."

He hung up the receiver, smiled faintly at Jo Gar.

"It was Señor Craise—asking for news," he said. His eyes fell on the collapsed figure. He spoke sharply to the Filipinos, telling them to take him to a cell.

They half dragged the man to the door. Jo Gar stood aside, frowning. Arragon was smiling broadly. He rubbed his browned hands together. There was the sound of clattering as the Filipinos dragged the prisoner down the narrow stairs that led to the corridor through which they would walk to the cells.

"It is well we were not too hasty with Señor—"

Arragon's voice died. A strangled scream sounded from below. There was a heavy thud—the sound of a body falling. Jo Gar jumped towards the door. The wooden stairs had a landing half way down—the remaining steps were slanted in the opposite direction, hidden from his sight. There was a low groan—another crash of a body going down. He could hear heavy breathing as he started down the stairs, Arragon at his heels. On the landing they turned, stared down.

One Filipino was on his knees, holding his head with both hands. Red stained the fingers. The other was lying motionless against the corridor wall, face downward. The screened door opening on the alley just off the Escolta.

The caleso, pulled by a sturdy horse, moved swiftly towards the Bay. It was a dark night; there was no moon. A hot breeze blew in from the direction of Cavite. The Luneta, flanked by the Manila Hotel and the Army and Navy Club, was behind now.

Jo Gar sat in the open carriage and fingered the Army Colt. His lips were pressed tightly together; he was frowning with narrowed eyes. The police search was being carried out along the big boat waterfront, not along the Pasig. Juan Arragon was thinking of the prisoner's word—"Let me go—into the Bay. The sharks—"

A broken man—a prisoner who had looked so much like an

important citizen of Manila, had suddenly, savagely twisted himself from the grip of the two Filipinos supporting him along the corridor. With one blow he had knocked one Filipino unconscious. As the other had reached for his short club the prisoner had battered him against the wall of the corridor, had jerked the club from his grip—and had struck him heavily over the head with it. Then he had made his escape. He had possessed the strength of a madman, truly.

The caleso driver pulled up the horse, twisted his brown face. Jo Gar paid the man, slipped from the carriage, moved swiftly towards the Bay. He kept close to an old stone wall on his right.

There were lights in the Craise house on the Bay. But the Island detective did not enter through the scrolled iron gate. He went through a narrow passage in the wall, moved through the heavy, tropical growth of the garden.

He circled the big house at the rear, reached the Bay side. Stars gave faint light to the water. In the distance he heard the muffled exhaust of a power boat. He halted, listened. The boat was going away—but it was not so far distant. He smiled grimly, moved more rapidly around the house. And then, crouched low and moving swiftly, he saw the figure that had left the sand behind and was coming towards the growth near the house.

Jo Gar waited, the Colt gripped in his right hand fingers. He could see the figure now—the man was ten feet from him. The Island detective spoke quietly, sharply: "Up—Donnell!"

The figure stiffened. Gar heard the quick intake of breath. And then the man leaped towards him.

Jo Gar stepped to one side. He struck outward and downward with the Colt. It battered heavily against the attacker's head, just over the left ear. The man dropped—rolled over on his back. He was motionless.

The Island detective drew a deep breath. He shifted the weapon, got a small flashlight from his pocket. When he looked down upon the figure there was a hard smile in his blue-gray eyes.

"Like many tremendous schemes, Señor Craise," he said very slowly, "it has failed."

Jo Gar let his eyes move from the figure of Juan Arragon to that of Arnold Carlysle. He was smiling cheerfully in spite of the heat in the police head's office.

"Señor Craise was always shrewd, cold," he said slowly. "He was not one to forget that Ben Rannis had struck his brother down. I do not believe too much in the similarity of humans. But he did fool me, in Juan's office. Belladonna to enlarge the eye pupils, dirt-matted hair, no erectness like that of himself. And the changed voice. Neither Juan nor myself knew him too well, you see. And he'd been away for months. This English friend of his who has confessed to imitating Craise's voice—that was a clever touch. Calling up, pretending it was Craise—with Craise passing as a beachcomber, right in Juan's office at the time. And it was this Condon who answered my call to the house, of course."

Juan Arragon nodded his head slowly. "Had Craise got back to his house we would have been beaten," he said. "He could have received me, immaculately attired. He would have been clean, changed. In a dark room I would not have noticed his eyes. But of course, after the escape, he realized I would be busy—and that would give him more time."

Jo Gar nodded. "He murdered Rannis, just as he as Donnell told us. He got back to the house from the murder in time to receive me. Your Filipino guard was not too good, Juan, though it is a large place for one man to watch. Craise went out again, after you released him. There was sufficient time. He went to the Pasig, crouched along the bank—and when your men found him he threw the knife away. Said he was Donnell—and looked—a beachcomber. After his escape he got to the big boat piers where he hid and waited. After dark Condon met him in a power boat. He brought him to the Bay house."

Arnold Carlysle smiled faintly. "But for you Señor Gar, we would have assumed that a man resembling Craise had tried a pretty plan and had failed. And had then preferred drowning—and the sharks."

Jo Gar said nothing. He wondered if Arnold Carlysle would not have preferred it that way. But it was not for him to say.

"I was suspicious," he said slowly. "Before I knew Rannis had been murdered, when I told Craise that—he was very startled. I was almost too soon for him. He hadn't expected it this fast. And then, very suddenly, he was too cool. He was thinking too much of the future, of the circumstantial evidence that he knew he could beat."

Arragon shrugged. "Death in the Pasig," he said slowly, "is always difficult." He smiled at Jo. "Not being a fool, I congratulate you."

Jo Gar fanned himself slowly with his pith helmet. He smiled in return.

"Perhaps I had the better opportunity," he said quietly. "But not being too modest—I am pleased. Señor Craise is not an inferior actor."

Carlysle frowned down at the polished floor of his office. Juan Arragon nodded agreement. Jo Gar closed his eyes, stopped fanning his browned face, and drowsed. He suddenly felt very weary.

THE LARS AND SHAINE CRIME TRILOGY BY ERIC BEETNER

"Like if you took Lawrence Block's famous hitman, Keller, and made him the lovechild of Elmore Leonard and Quentin Tarantino." —Criminal Element

BLACK MASK
The Richmond City Free Press

VOL. 1 — All the Stories from 1928 to 1930 — NO. 1

RAW LAW: THE COMPLETE CASES OF MacBRIDE & KENNEDY
VOLUME 1

BY FREDERICK NEBEL

INTRODUCTION BY DAVID LEWIS

Series Editor: Keith Alan Deutsch

Crimes of Richmond City

CAPTAIN STEVE MacBRIDE was a tall square-shouldered man of forty made of lean hard bitten years. He had a long, rough-chiseled face, steady eyes, a beak of a nose, and a wide, firm mouth that years of fighting his own and others' wills had hardened. His face shone ruddily, cleanly, as if it were used to frequent and vigorous contact with soap and water. For eighteen years he had been connected, in one capacity or another, with Richmond City's police department, and Richmond City today is a somewhat frantic community of almost a hundred thousand population.

Dog Eat Dog

WHEN CAPTAIN MacBRIDE was suddenly transferred from the Second Precinct to the Fifth, an undercurrent of whispered speculation trickled through the Department, buzzed in newspaper circles, and traveled along the underworld grapevine.

It was a significant move, for MacBride, besides being the youngest captain in the Department, he was hardly forty was known throughout Richmond City as a holy terror against the criminal element. He was a lank, rangy man, with a square jaw and windy blue eyes. He was brusque, talked straight from the shoulder, and was hard-boiled as a five-minute egg. Now the Second Precinct is in the very heart of Richmond City's nightlife, bigger an important and busy station. The Fifth is out on the frontier, in a suburb called Grove Manor, and carries the somewhat humorous sobriquet of the Old Man's Home. Plenty of reasons, then, why MacBride's transfer should have been made matter for conjecture.

MacBride said nothing. He merely tightened his hard jaw a little harder, packed up and moved. To his successor, Captain

The Law Laughs Last

TOUGH precinct was the Second of Richmond City, lying in the backyard of the theatrical district and on the frontier of the railroad yards.

A hard-boiled precinct, touching the fringe of crookdom's elite on the north—the con men, the night-club barons, and on the south, the dim lit,

Law Without Law

KENNEDY chuckled. "So—we're back in the Second, Mac."
"See me here, don't you?"
"Ay, verily!"
The old station-house, blown up during the last election, had been rebuilt, and the office in which Captain Stephen MacBride sat and Kennedy, the insatiable news-

New Guns For Old

ALTUS PRESS • THE NAME IN PULP PUBLICATIONS
Available at AltusPress.com and finer bookstores

As a short story writer, Jim Wilsky has published more than fifty crime stories, and his four book Ania series, written with collaborator Frank Zafiro—see "Adam Raised a Cain" earlier this issue if you're a reader who doesn't go in order—is being re-released in April from Down & Out Books, beginning with Blood on Blood. Jim's first solo novel is nearly complete and currently lives in the former Republic of Texas with his wife and two daughters.

Bear Trap
Jim Wilsky

Saturday, 10:45 p.m.
I park about a block away in a shopping strip parking lot. I never like to park on the street, any big street. It's a little rule of mine. Never good. I don't care what I'm doing, where I'm at or even if I'm working. It just ain't smart.

I start down the darkened back alley that runs behind a few businesses until it gets to Czarnecki's. The storefronts are on Diversey Avenue but I don't want to go in that way unless I have to. It's still damn hot, even at this time a night, and I'm sweating like a bastard. Chicago's been an oven all summer. Seems like every fuckin' day it's been in the high nineties and the humidity's been through the roof since early June.

I was supposed to have been here an hour ago but that's okay, they said they'd wait for me after they closed up tonight. Patrik asked me to drop by and check out what was going on. I said sure, glad to help. I told him I knew the family and they've known me forever. It was no problem. He also wanted me to make sure that they understood that if they needed help with somebody, it ain't free.

This whole thing is a step up for me. I just turned twenty, but it's an old twenty. I've seen and done some things. Been around the block a few times if you know what I mean. But this ain't some convenience store robbery. This is some real business. I'll earn some cred doing this favor for the Dudeks.

Word gets around, people talk. Even back when I was in high school, I had a rep. I've always been known for leaning on some people pretty hard and just beating the living fuck outta some others.

I get calls to do some work quite a bit these days. Sometimes I do it just because they ask, but more often they're giving me a price for collecting on a debt or a loan, some shit like that. I work by myself, I ain't in some gang and I'm not an organization goon. It can be little stuff for dimes or it can be bigger stuff for money that ain't too bad. Just depends. Let's put it this way—I got a car, an apartment and enough cash to throw around on weekends.

Czarnecki's Meat & Deli, owned and run by Piotr and his son Michael, is older than the ground it's sitting on. Been around since, I don't know, nineteen-o-somethin'. Same location and same family run business that it has always been. I still come here every once in a while for sausage or a maybe a few groceries but not near as much as I used to. My mother used to come here weekly and her mother before her. The place is an absolute gold mine, a cash cow, and always has been.

I try the back door and it's unlocked like it always was, until Piotr or Michael finally go home for the night. I walk right in and there is a long wood table. Behind it is a little sawed off bald guy, wearing a wife beater T-shirt and bloody apron. An earring catches the overhead fluorescent light.

He stops cutting the steaks he's working on and stands straight up, raising his butcher's knife slowly toward my abdomen. I smile at him and he just stares at me with dead, lidded eyes, cigarette off to one side of his mouth. He finally nods at me and waves the knife sideways towards the front of the store, then goes back to cutting. He must recognize me from when I used to come in more.

It's easy to hear Piotr and Michael—or Marek as his dad always calls him—up in the front of the shop. They've always talked like the rest of the world is fucking deaf. Both are speaking in loud and rapid fire Polish. Both bitching about the business. Prices are too high, prices are too low. We ran out of this, we got too much of that. We need to advertise more, we don't need to advertise so much.

On and on they go as I walk down the narrow hallway that leads to the front of the store.

I walk through the swinging aluminum door after them and there they are, nose to nose behind the large, glass and stainless steel deli display cases. Only a few of the lights are still on, so the small store is dim and shadowed.

The door to the backroom squeaks as it slowly rocks to a stop. They both stop talking and turn to look at me. Staring at me like I'm a ghost, mouths open. Funny as shit.

"Eh, ehhh!...Hold it the fuck down!" I grin at them. "Stop arguing...*przestańmy*!"

Old man Czarnecki shoots both arms straight up in the air like a referee signaling a touchdown. "Ohhh *Gówno*, Marek, look...look who's here!" Piotr's big smile shows brown, crooked teeth.

Michael, who's maybe twenty-three or -four, nods and simply says, "Jerzy." Then he gives me a small plastic smile.

"Hey, Piotr! How are you, you old fox?" I ask him. Always did like this old man and I walk towards him.

While I'm hugging his old man, I glare over his shoulder at Michael. The younger Czarnecki and I just don't click. Never have. He doesn't like me, doesn't like guys who break laws or rules and basically thinks I'm a dumb ass punk. Michael's just an arrogant college boy. He's always thought he's smarter than everyone else but he's still Piotr Czarnecki's son and he's still not in charge of the store, so he don't have any choice but to put up with me right now.

Michael walks over and gives me a quick, limp-ass handshake, then wipes his hands off on his apron. Like I'm dirty or diseased or something. "So, you must have got hired or maybe promoted up from assistant bouncer. You the big enforcer now, huh?"

"Hey, it's just me here." I hold my hands out but give him a fuck you look. "I got asked to come see what's going on, that's all. Plus it's been awhile since I been in here...and great to see you, too, *Mikey*."

"Your brother, uhh, Mick. Yeah, Mick. He still a cop, you know...doin' honest work?"

"He's my half-brother and yeah Mike, he is. Saving the world, every day. Protecting innocent women and children and well, college boys. You shoulda called him, I guess." I took a step closer to him. "He'd a rolled up, wrote some bullshit notes down and promised to *look into this* for you."

"I would have called him, if I had any say in the matter."

He sticks his chin out and bows up on me a little bit.

"And nothing would've happened...nothing but another report filed. I mean Pollacks have never exactly been on the top of an Irish cop's to-do list. Especially when nothing has really even happened yet, right? Chicago PD wouldn't show up until something has *already* happened. But you're a smart guy Mikey, highly educated. You surely know all of that?"

He ignores my question, shaking his head. "Jerzy Sawyer. That name has always cracked me up. Just sounds, I don't know, wrong," Michael says with a shit-eating grin. He adds a smart ass chuckle. "It just sounds funny, you know?"

"No, man, I don't know." I laugh with him but also at him. "And, hey, you want to watch yourself here, okay? I mean, you don't want to end up head first in one of those dumpsters out back, spittin' rotten cabbage leaves out." I'm smiling but it's really more of a sneer. "*You know?*"

Michael's smile kinda melts away as Piotr gets in between me and his son. "Okay, okay now. Both of you, stop this bickering. I swear to God in heaven you're just like two little boys."

"Yeah. Yeah, sure, Piotr. Sorry about that." I drag my look away from Michael over to his dad. "So tell me what the problem is. Tell me what's goin' on here?"

Old Man Czarnecki puts his hands on his hips and grins. "Eh, no more *Rosjanie* problems with you here, Jerzy. I know you'll take care of this thing." He shoots his son a disgusted look. "Poles must always stick together," he says, warning Michael with his eyes."

"Russians? They botherin' you, huh?"

"Jerzy...for three weeks now." Piotr holds up three bony fingers. "A couple of them have been coming by. Snooping around, eating free samples, scaring our customers. They've been saying we need to be careful, saying we are going to get robbed. Telling us the neighborhood is dangerous these days and we need their help." He shakes his head and continues, "Then yesterday the Bear, that Skansi guy, came with them. That's when I called Ambrozy."

"Fuckin' *Rosjanie*. They're pigs, I hate 'em all." Trouble is, I have no idea who exactly he's talking about. "They won't ever just stay with their own. What's this Skansi guy's full name? And who, or what is this Bear thing?

"I'll be right back, Tata." Michael walks to the front door of the shop. It has big top and bottom bolt locks and a regular handle lock. He checks them all. "I'm gonna go back there and help Tomasz cleanup. He should be done cutting by now and we can finish grinding tomorrow. You need to get home anyway."

Piotr nods to his son and then looks back at me. He shakes his head again and frowns. "His name is Bogdan. Bogdan Skansi, the son of Viktor."

"Well, I've heard plenty of stories about Viktor Skansi down through the years. I mean shit, everybody has. He's been in Chicago forever, right? Like since before I was born?"

"Oh *tak*, way before. He came here as a young boy, with his family. They immigrated here from Ukraine, way back in the sixties." Piotr reaches into a high cupboard filled with bowls and plates. It also has a bottle of Smirnoff.

He finds two juice glasses and fills them less than halfway as he keeps talking. "So yes, Viktor is an old Russian goat...but a powerful old goat. He's left the country, gone back to Kiev for a while from what I hear. He had a big problem with taxes...but he also had a daughter named Misha get into trouble. Her boyfriend got her messed up on drugs. She tried to kill herself. He was some state senator's son, a rich boy from Lincoln Park." Piotr's eyebrows raise and he rubs his finger and thumb together, making the money sign.

It makes me laugh and I ask him, "Yeah, okay. So what happened?"

"Rich boy disappears. They never did find him. But the rumor was Viktor killed the boyfriend himself. No charges were ever filed but the case remained opened and the cops turned up the heat on Viktor. Everyone knew that it was most likely Viktor that had done it." Piotr shrugs. "Maybe him and Bogdan, who knows, eh?"

"How you know so much about him, Pollack?" I ask him and grin, taking the glass he holds out to me.

"Ahh, you're forgetting, Jerzy. Decades ago, I committed the unforgivable sin of marrying a Russian girl." He has a grim look on his face but only for a second, then he laughs. "Tatiana knows everything about everybody, but she's also the reason for all my Skansi problems." He lets out another laugh and slaps my shoulder.

"Oh shit, yes, your Russian princess. I did forget that." I put the glass out to Piotr and he clinks it. We both drink. "So that's good, eh? Old Viktor is gone."

"No, not good. In his father's absence, Bogdan is out to prove himself worthy of taking over the organization someday. While the old man is away, he's scratching and scraping for any extra money he can get. More drugs, more prostitution, bribery, extortion…anything and everything he can get his hands on to control and increase the money flow into the Skansi mob."

I nod to Piotr while remembering how much Ambrozy Dudek had always complained about the Russians trying to take business away from him and eat away at his territory.

"But Jerzy, this Bogdan is not just overly ambitious, he also has no respect for the old ways. He doesn't care how or what he has to do to achieve these things. There has been killing going on and families being threatened." Piotr takes another drink and I notice his hand is shaking a little. Could be fear, could be just a spell of the old age shakes.

"Yeah, when Patrik told me to come talk to you and see what's up, he also told me to be careful. That must be who he was talking about?"

He nods at me. "Even Viktor had his own set of rules. He would break them from time to time, it was his nature, but not like his son. Bogdan is a very bad man. Brutal, no heart, no soul. Nothing is out of bounds for him, you know?" Piotr's voice had gotten shaky too. Patrik's warning to be careful echoes in my head, but fuck that and fuck this Bogdan guy too.

I take a quick glance out the big front window of the shop. It's late, stores and shops across the avenue are dark. Very little traffic and empty sidewalks. I turn back to Piotr but as I do, movement catches my eye. A car glides into view, driving slow, I mean like real slow. It's a shiny new black Mercedes. It almost comes to a stop and I can feel eyes on me but then it rolls on out of sight.

The door to the backroom squeaks and swings open. My eyes flick to the noise and movement while my right hand goes behind me to the small of my back.

"All cleaned up back there, *Tata*," Michael says coming out into the front of the store again. "I sent Tomasz home. We need to go too. It's late. Let's get you home."

"Yes, Marek. We'll go." Piotr looks at me and smiles. "Ahh, Jerzy, I'm a tired old man and the walk home isn't getting any shorter for me these days."

They live about four blocks away, in the house they've always had. A house that was once owned by Piotr's father. They just walk to work and back home. Every day and every night. Not good with this kinda shit goin' on.

"Okay, listen, Piotr, I'll have a talk with Patrik and Ambrozy tomorrow morning." I shrug and move towards the back room with them. "See how they want to handle this thing. We'll fix this. Don't worry about money or anything, I'll tell them we need to help you out this one time...no strings. I'll talk to them about that too."

Right on cue, Michael looks at his dad and shakes his head slowly. "Fix this? They'll be back and then we'll have to pay Ambrozy *and* the Russians. Both. You watch, *Tata*."

The old man holds a hand up to silence his son, then he walks to the meat case and slides it open. "Tell Ambrozy thank you." He pulls out two big loops of fresh Kielbasa while he's talking. Tearing off some white butcher paper, Piotr wraps and tapes it up. He hands it to me and says, "You tell him thank you, for me. You tell him Piotr Czarnecki says that to him, okay, Jerzy? Tell him *dziękuję*."

Outside in the alley, Michael shakes the back door he just locked and turns to me. "We can't pay for protection. We *won't* pay for protection. Do what you need to do to convince the Dudeks of that."

"So, you weren't listening to me. I already said that I'd take care of the money." I step up close to Mike again and picture in my mind laying his ass out right here. I won't do it though, wouldn't be the right thing to do in front of Piotr.

Michael doesn't say another word, he just takes his dad's arm and aims him down the alley. They walk away and I let them go until they get close to rounding the corner before I start walking too.

Over his shoulder, Piotr calls out to me, "Thank you, Jerzy. Let us know something tomorrow, eh?"

"I will, Piotr."

The entire way to their house, Michael, being the dumbass he is, doesn't even glance behind them. Instead of me, it could have been somebody else walking behind them. Somebody that didn't have their best interests in mind, let's say. I follow them all the way too, because I keep thinking of that shiny black Mercedes. Didn't see it again the whole way, barely saw any cars at all.

When I see the Czarneckis climbing their front stoop, I peel off and start walking back to where I parked earlier. I look at my phone and see that it's almost midnight.

I need a drink. I got plenty of time for a couple over at the Copper Top lounge, they're open until three or some shit. It's only a five minute drive from here. No one is ever in that dive and that's the way I want it right now. Besides, I got nothin' to drink at home except out of code milk. That's the truth. The inside of the fridge looks like the rest of my damn apartment. Empty and cold.

Sunday, 6:20 a.m.
I wake up early like I usually do and walk into the kitchen, which is also my living room. That's it too, except for my ten by eleven bedroom. Efficiency apartment my ass, it's more like a walk-in closet.

Better this than living with Gar and my crazy mother. As soon as I was able I got the hell out of that madhouse. I dropped out of high school my senior year, took what little shit I had and never looked back. Dad got sent up about a year after that. He's doing time in Wisconsin Columbia Correctional, I think it's called. North of Madison, middle of fuckin' nowhere. But, hey, whatever. I need coffee bad. There is just enough left to make a pot and I get it started. I sit at a folding card table that passes as a kitchen table and wait. *Fuck* I'm hungry, and my stomach growls to confirm it. I think I'll go get some breakfast.

I hear my phone chirping back in the bedroom and find it on the dresser. Looking at the screen, I don't recognize the number but I answer anyway, mostly just so I can hang up on whoever it is.

"What?"

"Jerzy? Hey. Whaddya mean 'what'? The hell kinda way is that to answer the phone?" Patrik sounds all business, no kidding around.

"Jesus, what're you doing up? You should just be going to bed." I walk back to the kitchen to get some coffee whether it's done or not. "I mean shit, I get up early and all but I don't talk early…need coffee. I'll call you back in like, I dunno, half hour…Okay?"

"You can drink and talk at the same time." He is definitely edgy. "We're gonna talk right now. This is important."

"Alright, alright. Hold on a second." I rinse out a cup that's sitting on the counter with the other dirty dishes. The coffee isn't done brewing yet, so while I'm pouring a cup real quick it drips and sizzles on the hot plate.

Patrik is in no mood for waiting. "After you called me last night from that bar and told me what was going on with Czarnecki's...I talked to Ambrozy."

"Yeah, okay." I take a sip of the coffee, it's weak but at least it's hot. Too damn hot. "So whaddya want me to do? How can I help?"

"You can't. Not with Bogdan, anyway."

"What? Wait a minute..."

"Skansi is doing shit like this all over town. It's a big power move and we're stretched too thin to put out all the fires right now. We need to do some recruiting and it'll take some time before we can really push back. Week or two, probably more."

"Yeah, well, recruit me. I told Piotr we'd take care of this shit for him. Two weeks is a long time for him to stand around with his thumb up his ass."

"Ambrozy likes you, Jerz, always has since we was boys, eh?" Patrik's tone of voice went a little bit softer. "You and I, we go way back you know? You're like another son to Ambrozy."

"I know. So he should know he can trust me."

"Got nothing to do with trust. He wants you to get some experience under your belt and he's got big plans for you. You go after Skansi yourself and it won't turn out good for you. Ambrozy don't want you dickin' around with Bogdan direct. Now, if you can manage to send some messages to one or two of his boys...hey." I can almost see his shoulders shrug.

"Whoa. Hey. Just hold the fuck on." Now I do take a gulp of coffee, don't care how hot it is.

"No, you will hold on. You will listen now and let me finish." His voice goes back to hard and pissed off.

There is just silence from his end for a second but I don't jump in to fill it.

"Yes?" he finally said.

"Sure, Patrik, sure." I finished the coffee and poured more.

"These Russians, these bastard sons of whores, they are not well organized. Not as organized as we are...but they make up for it in other ways. They have no fear, they're not rational. They use brute force, not persuasion and kill without hesitation. Especially Bogdan."

"Look, I underst—"

"Stop talking. You understand nothing."

And you know what? I do stop but he's like the only guy in this city I would take that from.

"Listen to me now. We will handle all of this in due time. Old man Skansi has big problems with the feds and the Chicago PD, that's why he left the country. We have it from a valuable source that the case may involve Federal income tax evasion. Bogdan is out of control while his dad is gone. For now, he's in charge and he's grabbing everything he can, while he can. Big money or small, he doesn't care."

I hear Patrik shuffle the phone around. "Hold on, Jerzy." In the background, I can hear a muffled conversation in Polish.

"All right, I'm back. For now anyway, Ambrozy does not want to stir the pot. He wants to let Bogdan keep drawing the attention of law enforcement, attention the Russians already have. Bogdan is not too smart. Maybe he hangs himself. We stay out of it and don't muddy ourselves...for now. Except for lower level guys, if you can swing it."

He paused for a second and I jumped at the opening. "Patrik."

"Yes?"

"Can I ask you a quick question?"

He actually gives me a low chuckle on that. "I think I'm done for now. What is it?"

"How many guys does Bogdan have working for him? I mean guys that hang close to him. Small army, ten, five...what?"

"They are not big in numbers yet, but they will be someday. As I said though, they are brutal. Kill you in a blink and the worst of them all is Bogdan himself. I would say his main guy is a big animal named Anatoli Kartoff. Rarely do we see one of those two without the other. Bogdan probably has four of five other high level guys scattered around town. We do not know the precise number of soldiers he has working the streets."

He pauses for only a second and he ain't chuckling anymore. "But remember, Skansi is none of your concern. You did what we asked and you'll get something for that. If you have a little private talk with one or two of his guys, we'll take care of you for that, too."

"Okay, alright. I was just curious why this guy Bogdan would have bothered visiting Czarnecki's himself? Why not let this Kartoff asshole handle it? Or some other soldier?"

"Eh, that's why he's called The Bear. Sometimes bears don't do what you think they'll do. He's unpredictable, he likes to be seen and to be feared. Big ego. Tell you the truth, the Czarneckis have been lucky so far. Probably because of that Russian *kurwa* that Piotr is married to. She might be saving his ass right now and he doesn't even know it...Now, are we done? Have I been clear? Stay out of it, Jerzy. Tell me you will."

"I hear you loud and clear. I ain't in any rush to take a bullet."

"Yeah, yeah. Listen, I gotta go but Ambrozy would kill me if something happened to you. You are not ready yet for this Bogdan guy, okay? I know you, so give me your word, you prick. Now."

"Jesus. Okay, already."

There was a moment of silence from him then, "Alright, I'll be in touch."

I set my cell phone down and stare at it. Patrik is no dummy. There is a part of him that knows he might not have been successful with convincing me to stay away from Skansi and he knows I never really gave him my word.

Me? I see this as a great opportunity to get in even better with the Dudeks. I won't screw things up but they'll know it was me who stepped up and stepped in. I probably won't mess with this Bogdan fucker, though. I guess I can see the Dudeks' strategy there. Maybe.

The words *you are not ready yet* echo in my ears as I head in the bedroom to get dressed.

Tuesday, 11:47 p.m.
For all I know he's shacked up for the night with some whore but sometimes you just get lucky. I've been sitting in the parking lot of the Avondale Square apartment complex for almost four hours. The only light out here comes from the apartments' draped windows and tiny balconies.

There're two identical buildings, each three stories tall. I don't know Kartoff's actual apartment number but I was told this was the place and found out from Piotr that he drives that black Mercedes I saw at Czarencki's, so that's what I'm watching for.

After talking to Patrik yesterday morning, I did some homework and asking around. Mostly about Anatoli Kartoff but also anything I could get about Bogdan. Talked to Piotr again, talked to some guys I use to run with in high school. One of those guys has Russian blood but he was a little guy, pushed around by his own brothers, and he found a home when he hung out with us. Found out a little here and a little there.

Got some good physical descriptions on both Kartoff and Bogdan. Skansi, too. Kartoff is in his mid-twenties. A big boy. Goes six-three or six-four, weighs in north of two-thirty and he's got the build of a linebacker. He's known for carrying at all times and he isn't shy around a gun when he needs it.

I was told Bogdan is of average height. Right around five-ten, stocky and muscular. He just turned thirty. Evidently The Bear is a legend in fighting and it ain't just about bouncing people around. Word on the street is he's killed four or five neighborhood people. He's got short blond hair, wears earrings in both ears.

The best information I could get came from Piotr's busybody wife, Tatiana. Kartoff and Skansi are inseparable...except for Tuesdays and Fridays. Seems Skansi has a steady girlfriend north of the city, up in fuckin' Waukegan of all places. Bogdan drives himself up there. The girlfriend is a stripper at a joint the Skansies half own. When he's up there, the lovebirds stay at a lakefront summer cottage old man Skansi bought for a song back in the eighties.

Piotr told me his wife used to clean other people's houses for the extra money. One of her clients had been the Skansies, mostly the main house but sometimes the cottage as well. When her back started giving her problems and she gave it up, I guess the family may have taken it personal. Who knew what set these old world families against each other sometimes. The hell if I did.

It's Tuesday night now and while his boss is gone, I'm thinking on throwing a little surprise party for my man Anatoli. I'm gonna bust his ass up good if he ever shows up. Looks like that might not happen though.

Just as I'm thinking that a car turns down the street and lights up my interior. I crouch into my driver's seat and watch as the car slows, then sweeps into the same lot where I'm parked.

Bingo. In my rearview, I watch the Mercedes float by, looking for a parking spot. I'm carrying my favorite gun, a Beretta M9, just in case things go to shit. But that's not my first weapon of choice tonight. I pull out a blackjack from under my seat and get out.

I've got my phone to my ear as I walk through the lot toward Kartoff's car. It's dark but I don't see anyone else in there. As soon as he gets out and closes his door, I start having a fake conversation. He looks at me for a second then walks away toward his apartment building. The description was right. He's one big son of a bitch.

This ain't gonna be a fair fight, no golden gloves boxing match. This is a fuck you up message being sent. I close the gap between us, wind up and as he starts to turn I let him have it in the back of the head. There is a heavy crack as I make solid contact. He lets out a loud grunt and goes to one knee. I let him have it again from the side and this one catches him square on the ear.

He should have went down with either one or both of those hits but he didn't. The bastard somehow stands up, weaves a little, then lunges towards me with one hand going for his belt. Knife or gun I don't know because he never gets there. I hit him with another good one right across the forearm and I swear I hear his arm break.

Kartoff lets out a yell and he grabs at his busted arm with the other. I step in and kick the side of his right knee. It bends the wrong way and he screams. This time he does go down and tries to roll away from me. I give him a good kick in ribs, then another. As he protects his side, I follow that up with another roundhouse whack to the head with the blackjack.

Covering up the best he can with his face down, he groans and calls me a bastard through clenched teeth: "*Svoloch.*"

"Fuck you." I stand over him and hit his hands that are covering his head.

"*Poshel ty!*" he yells back what I just said to him. I hit him some more and I know I gotta be breaking bones in those hands 'cause I ain't holding back. Let's put it this way, he'll need somebody to tie his shoes for him for a long fucking time.

I can tell he's about had it but he actually rolls onto his back, with arms outstretched and crossed to block the blackjack. He's looking at me in the eye the best he can. The asshole is grinning, too.

Through the blood and pain, he's fucking grinning. "*Wiem, że.*"

He has switched to Polish now. Says he knows me. "*Wiem, że... Polack.*"

I straighten back up, wave the blackjack back and forth at him. "*Nyet,* Czarnecki's, *nyet.*"

Out of the corner of my eye I see some guy walk out of the apartment building in boxers and a T-shirt. He takes a few hesitating steps towards us, then stops. "Hey! Uh, hey, what's going on over there?"

I look at him hard and say, "You want some of this, ass-hat?"

The guy doesn't answer. Just holds up both hands shakes his head.

Kartoff wheezes and I look back down at him. He's still grinning up at me when he spits blood and almost in a sigh, breathes out my name, "*Dzhersi.*"

I should have killed the bastard right there but I need him to spread the news around, so I settle for beating the living shit out of him for another minute or so with the blackjack. I finally stop and look down at the mess I've left. I wipe the sweat from my forehead and look around. There's no one else around. Kartoff is no longer looking at anything, so I walk away. He's still breathing but he'll probably never be the same motherfucker again and that smile is sure as shit gone.

I walk to my car and get in. I see the neighbor guy come out of the building again, walk closer to the bloody body of Kartoff and then stare at the rear of my car as I back out. Fucker is no doubt getting my plate. I'm an asshole, should have covered it up. I wonder how screwed I am as I make the decision right then.

I ain't waiting around for the Russians or the cops—or both, to track my ass down. I'm leaving right now. Ten minutes later I'm on I-94 headed north out of the city. I'm going all the way on this. While I'm driving, I'll call Piotr Czarnecki.

Friday, 3:25 p.m.
I'm not a big planner and I seem to do better when I react on the fly. I knew how this thing was going to play out as soon as Patrik said I wasn't ready yet. The way I'm seeing it, at least right now, was that I'll lose the battle and pay for it, and I'll win the damn war later. The Dudeks might be pissed at first but they'll get over it fast

because when the dust settles, the Russians will be weak as shit and the blame won't be on Patrik or Ambrozy.

When I got up here two days ago, it was no problem finding the cottage with the address Piotr's wife had supplied. I found a cheap ass little motel that was real close to the place. Just a short walk, then cut through a park that's on the shoreline and I'm there.

I checked in with a fake driver's license I've had for a few years and paid them cash in advance for three days.

The hardest part has been the waiting around this cottage for these last couple of days and even though it's finally Friday, I'm still waiting. I broke in last night. Came through a screened in porch out back. Easier than hell, no alarm system. Only thing is, I'm tired as shit, haven't slept at all. Can't afford to. Gotta watch for them. I want her to get here first, then him. Otherwise my plan will have to change. If it's him, bang bang and I'm gone. With her first, it's better because of the story she'll tell.

I have the front drapes open just enough to see the rock driveway coming up to the cottage. I'm sitting in a small living room, there's also a separate kitchen and dining room with a short hallway that leads to one bath and two bedrooms. The road out front is a quiet little street. All these houses are small summer places but have over sized lots and big trees.

It's already getting dark, the day is slipping away and I'm starting to wonder if I fucked up here. I guess there's a chance Skansi won't stick to the normal schedule because of him getting all hinky and paranoid about what happened to his right hand man. But my money is still on routine and habit. Plus from all I've heard, he don't sound like the hunker down type.

And just like that, a brand new cherry red Camaro comes into view. It pulls into the drive. I stand up and go to the side of the bay window for a better look. So far so good, because it's her. She gets out, reaches into the back and gets two sacks of groceries. Long dark hair, young and oh yeah, hot to be sure. Short shorts and a tight low cut T-shirt are showing off the goods. She kicks the door shut with one foot and heads for the front door.

I hear her working the keys in the lock and then shuffle around the groceries as she comes in.

I'm waiting for her in the kitchen and when she sees me, her eyes get big. She drops one of the sacks and something inside shatters.

The girl wants to scream but all that she's able to get out is a whimper.

"You scream, you die." The ski mask I got on is probably scaring the shit out of her. It's already itchy and hotter than hell. "In the bedroom, now." I wave my gun towards the hallway.

She stumbles backwards with her hands out in front of her, hits the wall and knocks a small picture off the wall.

"Go. Now." I grab her arm and shove her out of the kitchen and into the spare bedroom. I don't have much time. Who knows how close Bogdan is to pulling in that driveway.

"*Please*!...oh please. Don't hurt me!" Her voice is a whisper. She's shaking.

I've got everything ready in the bedroom and tie her to the bedposts with drapery cords. But before I slap some duct tape on her mouth, I need to have a quick talk with her to make this work.

"Please...don't—" She's crying pretty good now.

I put on my best Italian mob guy accent. "Where's the snort? Where's he keep it?"

Her eyes show only confusion and terror. She shakes her head no. "What?...Wait...What do you mean?"

"Bogdan screwed me over on a coke deal. He owes me two fuckin' bricks and I'm here to collect. Where's he keep the shit? I know it's here." I level the gun at her. "Where da fuck is it?"

She's sobbing, trying to catch her breath. "We never have drugs here. I been clean for a year and he never does anything around me." Her teary eyes bore into me. "I swear it. Don't kill me, take what you want just don't kill me."

"Where is he?"

"I...I don't know...he said he wasn't coming." Her eyes give her up though as they dart to the bedroom door and back to me again. She's lying but tries to recover when she adds some more bullshit, "but I've got some friends coming over."

I lean in close to her. "Damn, you even eighteen? What's your name?"

"Amy...Please, I'll do anything."

"You're not from around here are you?"

"I...I'm from Tennessee."

"Man, I love that accent. I'm gonna cut you a break, honey. I got no beef with you. I'm not even gonna hurt you a little bit. You need to go back home and get yourself away from shit like this. This ain't your world, sweetheart."

She nods. I stand up, tear off some tape, and stick it across those pretty lips.

I walk to the door and turn back to her. "I'm going, but you tell Bogdan, I'll be back to settle things with him. Tell him Tony C. from the West Side was here to collect. Tell him he should never fuck with a Sicilian."

I walk out and close the door. As soon as I do I tear off the ski mask to cool down and stuff it in my front pocket. I don't waste any time getting back to the front window. House is too dark so I hit a few lights on the way.

A few cars go by, then nothing for a while but the wait isn't too long. Only twenty minutes or so after tying Amy up, a silver Lexus turns in the driveway. There isn't quite enough daylight for me to see, but it's gotta be him. If he brought somebody with him then all bets are off but fuck it, I'm ready.

There is a small closet near the front door and I wedge myself in, closing it easy.

The front door isn't locked and maybe she usually locks it after her, but too late now. I hear him work the doorknob and come in. Door shuts. I wait for him to pass. I gotta admit, this is really tense shit. My first killing is like seconds away.

"Amy? Amy, where you at, baby?" His accent is clear but the English is good. "You didn't answer my call."

I hear him walk by on the wood floor.

"Hey, Amy-girl?" His voice holds a little suspicion to it and it sounds like he's far enough into the living room so I make my move. I come out of the closet, gun ready.

He's probably ten feet away and almost into the kitchen.

When he turns, his face has no expression, no surprise, no fear, it's just blank. I shoot him once, twice, while he's going for the gun I know is under the sports coat he's wearing.

First shot hits him pretty square in the chest, second misses somehow. He doubles over and makes for the kitchen. I shoot again and miss again, it splinters the door jamb just as he goes by. I hear him mumble a curse and growl with pain in there. Then a heavy thump and clang as he knocks something off the counter on his way down.

I ease up to the kitchen doorway and then get down one on knee. Edging slowly around the door frame, the first thing I can see is his feet and the toes of his shoes are pointing up.

I know the fucker isn't dead. Just know it. So I better my view just a little bit more. Looks like he's propped up against the dishwasher but I can't see anything past mid-thigh. This ain't the movies, so I take that shot and hit him just above the knee.

He yells out something in Russian and shoots blindly through the doorway, then I see a hand grab at his knee. Now's the time. I swing around further, able to see everything but his head and I put another one into his chest. The top half of him slides sideways to the floor and the gun drops out his hand.

Three or four quick steps in and I stand over him. I'm shaking a little bit and wired up big time. His body convulses and he lets out a gurgling sigh. His eyes roll upwards, real slow, to meet mine. His upper lip curls showing his teeth but he has no words. I don't say anything either, just lean down and put a final round in his temple.

Done. Time to fucking go. Dodging the blood I leave through the back porch door. I don't run, but it's damn hard not to. I was sloppy in there, too many gunshots and I wasn't sure how loud they were outside of the tiny house. As I go, I slip off the black golf gloves I been wearing for two days and shove them in my back pocket. The little park next to the cottage is not lighted and I don't see anybody either. No dogs barking, porch lights coming on, or any of that kinda shit.

The walk to the hotel takes me five minutes. It's the longest five minutes I ever remember. Then I see the place and my car but damn it feels as if I'm moving in slow motion and I'll never get there.

When I do, I collapse into the front seat and start the car. That's when I realize I've been holding my breath for a while, maybe since the cottage. I need to force myself to take a deep one.

As I turn onto the interstate ramp heading south back to the city, I check the rearview out of habit. I know I'm clear and all but I know I'll keep looking all the way back to Chicago.

I don't feel good about killing Bogdan Skansi but I ain't too broken up over it either. The adrenaline is gone now and I'm running on empty. I'll sleep like a baby tonight if I can make it that long.

Tomorrow, instead of waiting for Chicago PD to yank my ass in

BEAR TRAP

for Kartoff, I'll go and turn myself in. You know, I'll be feeling all guilty and remorseful and shit.

Depending on how bad the beating turned out and if they don't decide to go for an attempted murder charge, I might only get three to five or something just long enough. Hard to say. I do know I'll be a model prisoner, a regular choirboy while I'm in. It'll be okay.

No one in the Czarnecki family will ever say a thing about this Bogdan deal to anyone, except that Piotr will tell Patrik the real scoop. That's just how it is. I don't have to worry about that. I'm part of something bigger now.

That's what I meant about losing this battle but winning the war. It'll be worth it someday.

Like the saying goes, you wanna play, you gotta pay.

TITLES BY
ANGEL LUIS COLÓN

A SONG OF PISS & VINEGAR SERIES   SHORT STORIES   NOMINATED FOR AN ANTHONY AWARD!

Our second Texan author this issue, Michael Bracken has won several Derringer awards for his fiction, including the Edward D. Hoch Golden Memorial Award for lifetime achievement. He's written over fifteen hundred short stories, edited numerous anthologies, and has been active in organizations like the Mystery Writers of America, Horror Writers of America, the Private Eye Writers of America, and the Science Fiction and Fantasy Writers of America. Don't ask me where he gets all his time from, I haven't a clue. Maybe it's a Texas thing...? "Texas Sundown" is the first of his stories we're lucky enough to publish here at the magazine.

Texas Sundown
Michael Bracken

I rolled into the West Texas town in the back of a beat-up Ford F-100, climbed out of the dusty red pickup when the driver stopped to refuel at the two-pump Conoco station, and stood clutching my olive-green canvas duffel bag. I brushed my hand through my flattop, knocking loose more dirt than dandruff as I took in my surroundings—the deserted main street, the empty diner across the way, the bank on the corner.

"Thanks," I told the driver.

The old man grunted in response.

I crossed over to the diner, settled at the counter on the stool furthest from the door, and placed my duffel at my feet. In it were a change of clothes, a full-face wool ski mask, a sawed-off double-barreled shotgun, and half a box of shells.

The brunette behind the counter watched as I settled into place. Like a sports car fresh from the showroom floor, she was hitting on all cylinders and I was ready to drive. Her pale blue uniform was buttoned up the front, had white trim around the short sleeves, and revealed more female thigh than I had seen in years. Hair parted in the middle had been pulled back into a ponytail that hung halfway down her back. Trying to impress a ponytail with a penchant for chocolate had been my first mistake. She asked, "What can I get you, Ace?"

"Anyone else here?"

She looked me up and down. "Cook doesn't come in 'til the dinner rush."

I wondered how many diners constituted a rush. "When's that?"

She glanced at the wall clock. "'Bout an hour."

I glanced at the clock. A quarter to three. I had time.

"I can fix anything you want." As I listened, I realized she lacked a Texas twang.

"Coffee," I said. "And a slice of that cherry pie."

She filled a chipped white mug with coffee so thin I could see the stains on its bottom, and a moment later slid a matching white plate across the counter to me, the slice of cherry pie oozing red like fresh road kill. I poked at it with my fork, tasted it, and pushed it away.

"Problem with your pie?"

"The coffee, too," I said.

I'd eaten better at Joliet, where I'd served time for a candy-store heist gone wrong and spent my waking hours dreaming of the Pacific Ocean. A week after my release, a former cellmate recruited me for a sure-fire bank job, a job that disintegrated into chaos when a dye pack exploded and bathed the two inside guys with red dye and tear gas. The getaway driver panicked and popped the clutch, killing the stolen Ford's engine. Rather than stand on the sidewalk with my thumb up my ass waiting to see what happened next, I hied off down the nearest alley, pulled off my mask and tucked my shotgun under my trench coat. When I exited onto the next street I caught a cab to the rooming house, shoved everything I owned into my bag and lit out of town in a stolen AMC Rambler Classic. It broke down near Springfield. Rather than risk attracting more attention by stealing another car, I thumbed it, heading southwest into Texas until I had a straight shot west to Southern California. I slept when I could and caught meals between rides.

"You see a better place to stuff your pie hole," the waitress said, motioning toward the door, "be my guest."

I stared at her, and she at me, and when I let my gaze drift I discovered her name was Claire. I asked, "You got cream?"

She pushed a creamer across the counter, and I used its lukewarm contents to top off my coffee. Then I added two sugar cubes, stirred, and sipped from the mug.

"Anything else?"

I shook my head and a moment later she slid a handwritten ticket facedown across the counter. I flipped it over and looked at the total. I didn't have enough change in my pocket to pay it even if it had been worth the price. I asked, "Where you from, Claire?"

"Rockport, up near—"

"Chicago," I finished. Though I didn't, not really, I said, "I know it."

"I blew in here six weeks ago," she said, "with nothing but an empty gas tank and a strong desire to eat. Owner gave me three hots and a cot in the back room."

I didn't ask what she had to do for the meals and the room, but I knew it wasn't just slinging hash. Instead I asked, "You got a car?"

"Out back."

I held out my hand, palm up. "Give me the keys."

She eyed me hard. "Why?"

I grabbed her arm and pulled her to the counter.

Claire didn't wince or flinch. She asked, "Where you headed?"

"West," I said. "The Pacific Ocean."

"Take me with you," she said. "I got nothing keeping me here."

"That bank—" I nodded through the window toward the corner, "—there any money in it?"

"Ought to be. Far as I can tell everybody in the county banks there."

I glanced at the clock. "Get your things, then. It's time."

Claire grabbed her purse and cleaned out the register. Then she grabbed something from under the counter and shoved that in after the cash. On the way out back she stopped in the storage room long enough to fill a small suitcase. Outside, she threw her purse onto the front seat and her suitcase into the rear seat of a black two-door Ford Falcon before climbing behind the wheel.

As she started the engine, I climbed in and pushed her heavy purse across the bench seat toward her. I pulled my clothes from the duffel bag and tossed them into the back with Claire's suitcase. Then I loaded the sawed-off shotgun, put extra shells in my pocket, and pulled the wool ski mask over my face.

"Pull up in front of the bank and keep the engine running," I instructed. "Be ready to go as soon as I come out."

"Which way?"

"West," I said. "Always west."

Claire did as instructed, and I was out of the car and inside the bank in a matter of moments. The bank had an elderly teller with a lacquered gray beehive filing her nails at one of the two teller windows, a pudgy bank manager thumbing through a girlie magazine at a desk near the entrance, and no guard.

The manager wore a blue pinstripe suit over a yellowing white shirt stretched tight across his ample abdomen, the collar unbuttoned, and the knot of his tie pulled loose. He looked up when I entered. Before he could react to my presence, I smashed the shotgun's grip into the side of his head and dropped him to the floor.

The teller dropped her nail file and her hands headed under the counter.

"Hands back up where I can see them, grandma!"

She did as instructed.

I put my duffel bag on the counter. "You know which one's the dye pack," I said. "So break the bands, throw the cash in loose. You're going to carry this out the door, so you pick the wrong one and you'll be painted red."

The teller pulled the cash from her drawer, breaking currency bands as she went and shoving loose greenery into my bag. She tossed one banded stack aside and then, while staring directly at me, shoved another under the waistband of her skirt and out of sight, her glare challenging me to complain.

I didn't. I smiled.

When there was no more cash in her drawer and she showed me that the other teller drawer was empty, I had her heft the bag and walk ahead of me out of the bank.

Nothing exploded.

I took the money from her, threw it into Claire's Falcon, and followed it in. When I turned back to the teller, she winked and slowly collapsed to the sidewalk as if she had fainted.

Claire accelerated away from the curb as soon as my butt hit the seat, and the sudden forward movement caused the door to slam. We were long past the Conoco before I realized no one had sounded the bank's alarm.

I opened the duffel bag and counted the money as Claire sped west, surprised at how much we had. After a bit, I said, "There's almost seven thousand here."

"That's a lot of coffee and pie," she said.

Claire kept glancing in the rearview mirror but no one followed us. Soon we relaxed and she slowed so we wouldn't attract attention from Highway Patrol officers working speed traps along our route.

"Why California?" she asked. "What's there for you?"

"I've never touched the ocean," I explained, "but I've seen it in movies." I told her about the Frankie Avalon and Annette Funicello beach movies I watched before my incarceration and told her I wanted to see the Pacific Ocean before I died. "What about you? What's there for you?"

"It isn't what's there," she said, "it's what isn't. There's nobody who knows anything about me or my past, and with the money we just took, there's no reason they ever will."

She wouldn't tell me what she'd done in Rockport that she wanted to put behind her, so I told her why I'd left Chicago.

When I finished she said, "Figured it was something like that, Ace."

Claire didn't say much else, and we chased the setting sun until nearly eight o'clock. I told her we needed to stretch our legs, but I wanted to do more than that. I wanted to celebrate.

At a campground exit, she left the state highway and drove up the side road until it dead-ended in a long-abandoned campground overlooking a reservoir.

She shifted the Falcon into park and let the engine idle.

I leaned over, grabbed her chin, and turned her face so that I could plant my lips on hers.

She resisted.

"Come on, baby," I said. "After all this, you're not going to deny me, are you? I know you're just as juiced as me."

Claire grabbed her purse from the seat between us, pulled out a snub-nosed .38, and pressed it into my belly. "Get out," she said. "Leave the money."

"No," I said. "You wouldn't."

She pulled the trigger. My ears rang. I felt a burning sensation in my gut, and I looked down at blood oozing out like that damn cherry pie filling. I tore the gun from Claire's hand and pounded her face with the butt until I felt faint and dizzy from lack of blood.

Then I stared west, into the sun as it set over the lake, until the ringing in my ears sounded like approaching sirens. I would never watch another beach party movie, never reach California, and never touch the Pacific Ocean.

I reached over, shifted the Falcon into gear, and pressed my left foot onto the accelerator.

THE JAKE DIAMOND MYSTERIES BY J.L. ABRAMO

"Abramo keeps the twists coming fast enough that readers have no choice but to keep turning pages."
—*San Francisco Chronicle*

"Abramo has the hard-boiled private eye formula down pat—solidly written and captures the mood of the genre."
—*Booklist*

S.A. Solomon is another short story virtuoso in what I think is a pretty stacked issue. I first met her at Noir at the Bar performances in Manhattan. When I see a story of hers in a magazine it's a difficult thing for me not to skip ahead and aim right for hers. But if that's you, don't do it. A lot of work goes into sequencing these things in the best order so march right back to the beginning, people. You'll get here, and believe me, it will pay off when you get here. Her stories always do.

Titan
S.A. Solomon

It would be the real estate broker who did him in—not so much the fact that she testified against him in court, which she did, her borough-girl-made-good accent mesmerizing the jury with multi-million dollar penthouse dreams—but she, herself, her cherry-tipped breasts, her quivering halves of canned peach butt cheeks cupped in a firm skin of expensive body girdling, her cloud of confounding scent like he'd collided with the perfume counter at Saks. His lawyer, Steigman, was gesturing with his Van Dyke beard, signaling him to focus on the tramp's testimony (scribbling on the white legal pad in defense attorney scrawl, PAY ATTENTION AS IF YOUR LIFE DEPENDS ON THIS). He was right, of course: it did.

Her name, she told him right off (like she would tell the jury, spelling it for the court reporter and the record), was B-U-N-N-Y P-A-P-P-A-S, Bunny Pappas, and she was from Queens.

Astoria, TBE (which she did not say to the jury but had purred breathily like she did all of her doublemint-flavored confidences into his large and sensitive ear). TBE? To Be Exact, she said, pinching his buttocks with each word for emphasis, making his face flare and his heart hammer against its ivory cage. What, in Jersey they speak properly, in full sentences your maw made you ask for your lunch money? And you didn't call her *maw*, you called her Mother, yeh? she chortled, diving back down into the rain forest of his crotch.

That afternoon had been the beginning of the end, when he had the cardiac event and she'd had to call nine-one-one, which he could tell colossally pissed her off because her royal highness the titular head of the agency would not tolerate scandal on company time, not from their highest-grossing broker for five, count 'em, five years in a row. Especially not when the emergency took place in one of the blue chip properties on which they had an exclusive listing.

B for B, as Bunny would say. What? he had pleaded as he spiraled into unconsciousness, what?

Bad for business, babycakes.

They were alike, he knew that, peas in a pod—the broker and the titan of industry—come up from the same squalling netherworld of crowded apartments and harried parents who worked themselves into a sickness for the promised but withheld fruits of this land. No immigration romance, that. Hard luck, harder lives, early deaths, and anger and want roiling beneath it all, which he became the magnet for, the smallest insubordination a capital crime that would have his father seething. He'd be banished from the dinner table or even the apartment, a smack in the head thrown in for good measure. He suspected she had similar stories, although neither of them had shared the details with the other. They just instinctively knew.

The titan was on trial for fraud, about to be brought low in a Manhattan courtroom gloomy even at high noon, the tarnished shades of disgraced corporate forebears swirling around the ceiling like cigar smoke in the paneled boardrooms he once dominated. He wouldn't be able to get Cubans in the pen. Maybe Steigman would send him a box to hand out to the various gatekeepers he was sure populated the prison. He would save one for himself and savor it secretly somewhere. Prison couldn't be that different from running a company. Everywhere had its CODB (now he was doing it), its Cost of Doing Business. It was just a matter of decoding theirs.

He learned that PDQ when he built that little Parsippany business, a manufacturer of industrial lubricants, into an empire. He'd landed a job in the sales department and worked his way up through the managerial ranks to become CEO, a master of acquisitions and organic growth, landing the company on the Fortune 500 list.

—Ahhh shit! A needling pain pulsed through the kid leather

cradling the arch of his foot where Steigman had stomped on it. Why in God's name was the shyster wearing roach killers? He immediately regretted the slur, a mental slip. Of course, he meant *counsel*, the strain was getting to him, that's why his father's rabid hatred of *etnics*, as he had called them—everyone who wasn't a Pole—rose in his throat like bile. His old man had despised them all: kikes, wops, chinks, spics, shades. Those prejudices had been instilled in him, and although he resisted, they had a way of reasserting themselves at stressful times, like now. He had been fifteen when the old man kicked off, knocked into purgatory by a forklift driven by one of the *etnics* (accidentally, they all swore) at the plant in Harrison where he had worked all his years since stepping off the boat. The son took a job at the factory—he was big for his age, and they knew his family needed the dough—but he didn't stay there. He was destined for bigger things.

He had to concentrate—it was not just his unfortunate mistakes that were on trial, but he himself, his life! He was already conceding defeat by picturing life "inside"—and that was not like him. To force himself to focus, like biting the soft tissues of his mouth, he pictured his wife, Sloane, impeccably dressed, freshly coiffed, sitting behind him in the courtroom together with the girls who were home on school break, a portrait of family support belied by the lawyer's letter she had left on his dressing table the morning he was scheduled to turn himself in. This carefully orchestrated charade of family support was in the settlement agreement Steigman's firm had negotiated.

Sloane wasn't leaving him because he'd cheated on her. She was divorcing him because his spectacular self-destruction was spread all over the tabloids, threatening her social standing. She came from the kind of family whose members sat on the boards of the city's storied cultural institutions, whose children took etiquette lessons and rowed crew and went off to boarding school. These things had always seemed foolish to him until he had daughters. He couldn't explain it, would have laughed outright if you'd told him his girls would be showing horses and attending debutante balls. But there it was.

He wasn't in the habit of cheating. It wasn't worth it for a high-profile corporate chieftain: the fallout would be more than personal, could affect share prices. It wasn't as if he hadn't had opportunities. Power—the kind that came from sitting on corporate boards, flying on company jets, collecting million-dollar bonuses—was catnip to women, he'd learned early on. (He had met Sloane at a charity ball, and her society upbringing hadn't prevented her from giving him a first-class blowjob in the powder room.)

But the sight of Bunny Pappas struck him like a thunderclap when they met in the lobby of the luxury building on Central Park West that summer day. His executive assistant should have been meeting the broker to look at corporate apartments, but she called at the last minute to cancel because she needed to be somewhere for her kid. Since he was in the neighborhood, he told her not to worry about it, that he would go instead.

He was that kind of boss, something nobody remembered when they made their deals with the prosecutor.

Bunny Pappas. A petite girl, perfectly proportioned, with succulent breasts and an ass to match. She was a class act, though, catering as she did to a high-class clientele. She wore high heels, tailored suits that accentuated her curves, and silk blouses buttoned just above her cleavage, where a coral pendant dangled like a fishing lure. She had long black hair that she wore up for business, down for trysts; petal-soft skin; pouty, kissable lips.

That day, that sultry summer day, she was wearing a silk sheath and the smell of honeysuckle drifted from her glowing skin. She hypnotized him. Her alert black eyes registered this fact, how he stammered and mumbled, his face reddening—he, who cowed corporate boards into doing his bidding and negotiated billion-dollar deals without breaking a sweat.

They didn't say much in the elevator to the penthouse floor. He was afraid his voice would crack like it had when he was thirteen, suffering from a crush on the landlady's daughter. He needn't have worried. Bunny Pappas had his number. She unlocked the apartment door, pushed him gently inside and, shutting the door behind them, unzipped his pants.

They looked at a lot of apartments over the next few weeks. They had sex in the master bedrooms of all of them. She explained that they were "staged" and nobody would be coming home to sleep in their rut-infused sheets but, he wondered, how many open houses had there been before him? ("Open house" was a figure of speech, since you had to have a minimum bank balance for entry.) She scoffed at his squeamishness and smiled wickedly as she pulled a silky throw out of her real estate agency branded tote bag. Something gave him the feeling she had done this before. But he didn't care. He would be the last, he was certain of that. And he was used to getting what he wanted.

That day of the cardiac event, the beginning of the end, they were discussing the interior design of the apartment he'd finally chosen, the one in the building on CPW where they'd first met and sparks flew. He didn't have the time to oversee the details, which were delegated to the decorator Bunny recommended to all her clients, a childhood friend of hers. The apartment was intended for corporate use and it was nothing for the titan to make a phone call authorizing a million-dollar wire to buy art and furnishings. He was aware that outrageous sums were being spent, but by then he was earning so much that it had almost become like play money. Besides, value had been transferred—it wasn't as if the expenditures were for his personal benefit. The apartment was an asset on the company books, used for business meetings. He had closed deals there, corporate acquisitions that he wanted to keep out of the public eye until negotiations were concluded and the ink dry. It was a discreet way to dodge the business press, which had a habit of taking note when a potential target company's CEO paid a visit with a retinue of investment bankers. This inevitably resulted in a news story the following day that was dissected by analysts and moved markets.

He let Bunny work out the details with the interior decorator, whose style was the opposite of the French antique collection his wife had amassed in their Park Avenue duplex and the house in Greenwich. It was like living in the Metropolitan Museum: he couldn't sit down. Bunny's decorator friend chose a minimalist approach featuring marble floors, chrome and leather daybeds, cool gray walls. She had her eye on a particular piece of art at auction. It was a bronze sculpture of an embracing nymph and satyr with a minimum bid that seemed awfully high. The designer assured him that the piece would appreciate in value.

Bunny liked it because she said it reminded her of the two of them. He placed a call. The wire was approved. Bunny summoned him to the apartment and, after an afternoon romp, informed him delightedly that they had made the winning bid on the sculpture. The decorator would arrange for its transport to the apartment after the appropriate amount of insurance coverage had been secured.

How much would that be? he asked lazily, his stocky frame feeling more pliable than it had in years, energized by the flow of post-coital endorphins pumping through his body.

Three million dollars, Bunny honked, unable to keep the Queens out of her voice.

She was surprisingly strong for such a little girl, dragging him out of the bedroom and into the foyer so the EMTs wouldn't find them *in flagrante*. She got his pants back on him in record time.

He survived, emerging even stronger, a new man once they put in a stent and the docs gave him his marching orders to eat right and exercise, things he'd always said he didn't have the time for. Now he saw that time was all he had, and he had to make it last. It didn't hurt that he could afford the best cardiologists and nutritionists and personal trainers.

Of course, the jury wouldn't hear about the circumstances of the cardiac event, not the buttock-pinching or silky sex sheets or master-bedroom monopoly. What in hell did he pay those shysters for if not to keep that stuff out of court? Infidelity on company time may look bad, but it wasn't illegal.

But some whistleblower, spurred by the promise of a government bounty, had spilled the news of the extravagant corporate art acquisition. The three-million-dollar bronze boner, as the tabloids salaciously described it, because, rather than "embracing" (as Bunny had so delicately put it), the mythological figures were fornicating.

That's when the vultures began circling, despite the fact that the company was strong in its fundamentals, its price-to-earnings ratio as sound as Manhattan bedrock. To add insult to injury, a muckraking journalist uncovered proof of other alleged improprieties in corporate spending proffered by a couple of disgruntled former employees (and weren't they all?).

The apartment in the luxury building on Central Park West became People's Exhibit 1.

Yes, Bunny Pappas had been B for B, bad for business, which became crystal clear the morning after her testimony, when the jurors filed into the courtroom and not one would meet his eye.

(But not bad for hers: she had gone on to succeed the head of the real estate brokerage which now bore her name.)

Bunny didn't look at him either, not because she felt bad about testifying, he thought, but because he could no longer meet the minimum balance requirement.

The jury was composed of ordinary people—with a few *etnics* thrown in, driving the forklift of justice, he noted despairingly. They were hypnotized by Bunny (he knew the feeling) but suspicious of him. He understood. He'd been in their shoes, once upon a time, if only they could see that. He'd thought that by testifying he could hammer that fact home, bond with the jury over his humble beginnings. But the more he spoke, the more he seemed to be digging his own grave. He perspired profusely, his face reddened, he sounded defensive and belligerent even to his own ears. He saw the jurors look incredulously at the judge, his lawyer, the assistant district attorney, the spectators—anywhere but at him. He could almost see the thought balloons popping up over their heads: "L-I-A-R."

He had to take a nitro pill when he got off the stand. A court officer escorted him to the toilet. There was no executive washroom in the courthouse. He used a rank-smelling stall with graffitied tips for bail bondsmen and phone sex hotlines. He dreaded returning to the courtroom where the jury would hand down his fate. He washed his hands thoroughly, eyeing the narrow window by the sink. He wouldn't even be able to get one shoulder through.

You're built like a bull, Bunny had cooed admiringly.

He was supposed to have paid attention during her testimony so that his lawyer could attack her credibility on cross-examination. Instead, he had lost himself in a reverie of frolics past. And anyway, what could he say in response to her allegations, both spoken and implied?

He *had* been seduced by her cherry-tipped breasts, her canned-peach butt cheeks.

He *had* been seduced by the Central Park West penthouse's exclusive views.

He *had* been seduced by the millions in annual bonuses, more money than these jurors would see in a million lifetimes.

It was no excuse to argue that everyone was seduced by these things, that it was the American dream to achieve them. It was his job to steer the ship, to stay the course, to be unmoved by the sirens' song.

To be the titan.

Sure, the amounts were sizeable, huge numbers, almost cartoonish, but he had earned them. Last year alone, the company had generated seven billion dollars in revenues, two billion in profits, and cash flow in excess of one billion. The business had booked twenty-four consecutive quarters of profit when he was CEO.

The company would surmount this, would triumph, would shake its flailing handlers, the forensic accountants and the lawyers, from its flanks like a mythical Titan, an immortal unbound by the commands of mere men.

He would have a lot of time to think about these things, he understood when the jury returned from the deliberations. The forewoman (a sour looking middle-aged gal), stood to drone out the verdict of guilty seventeen times for seventeen counts of fraud.

He was a titan no more.

Now he was just the guy with the three-million-dollar boner.

Next Issue

Next issue our featured story is by the writing team of Michael Stanley and their fascinating Botswanan character, Inspector Kubu. Their series is one of the very few that I can recommend to people without reservation. If you haven't encountered Kubu before, you're in for something special. I know people say that, but this time it's really quite true. Have a terrific spring!

Cheers,

On the following pages are a few
more great titles from the
Down & Out Books publishing family.

For a complete list of books and to
sign up for our newsletter,
go to DownAndOutBooks.com.

Texas Two-Step
Michael Pool

Down & Out Books
April 2018
978-1-946502-56-8

Cooper and Davis are a couple of Widespread Panic-obsessed Texas ex-pats growing some of Denver's finest organic cannabis. At least they were, until legal weed put the squeeze on their market. When their last out-of-state dealer gets busted, they're left with no choice but to turn to their reckless former associate Sancho Watts to unload one last crop in Teller County, Texas.

What ensues is an East Texas criminal jamboree with everyone involved keeping their cards so close to their vest that all the high-stakes dancing around each other is sure to result in bloodshed.

A Scholar of Pain
Grant Jerkins

ABC Group Documentation
an imprint of Down & Out Books
February 2018
978-1-946502-15-5

In his debut short fiction collection, Grant Jerkins remains—as the *Washington Post* put it—"Determined to peer into the darkness and tell us exactly what he sees." Here, the depth of that darkness is on evident, oftentimes poetic, display. Read all sixteen of these deviant diversions. Peer into the darkness.

I'm Not Happy Till You're Not Happy
Crime Stories by Ryan Sayles

All Due Respect, an imprint of
Down & Out Books
March 2018
978-1-948235-19-8

From a bank robbery gone horribly wrong to a shipwrecked man with a serious anger problem to a lonely teenage Peeping Tom, Ryan Sayles's second collection of stories steam rolls along.

Need a transvestite beating up her drug dealer? Got it. What about a guy trying to stuff a dead hooker into his trunk? Got it also. Need a Richard Dean Buckner story? Got two of 'em.

Come on in and join the mayhem.

Fast Bang Booze
Lawrence Maddox

Shotgun Honey, an imprint of
Down & Out Books
March 2018
978-1-946502-54-4

After seeing Frank deliver an impressive ass kicking in a bar fight, Russian mobster Popov hires him to be his driver. What Popov doesn't know is that when Frank is sober, he's inhumanly fast, deadly, and mute; when Frank is on the sauce, he's a useless twenty-something wiseass.

Double-crossed in a drug deal gone bad, Frank and Popov have one night to recover their stolen cash or get wiped off the map. Frank's special abilities put him in the spotlight, and he struggles to keep it all together…

Made in the USA
Las Vegas, NV
10 November 2021